PART ONE
THE RED HAND

1

Acknowledgments

For my mom, who has always told me to dream big!

To my team of editors and beta readers, you guys are awesome.

Last but not least, to my readers: thank you so much, and I look forward to many adventures together!

Be sure to check for updates and new book releases on my blog and Facebook page. Also, you can sign up for my newsletter on my blog to get the inside scoop and other goodies!

http://kaelynrossbooks.blogspot.com/

http://www.facebook.com/pages/Kaelyn-Ross/1570875296481518?ref=hl

Author's Note

Tribe - Part One: The Red Hand is a 35,000 word young adult dystopian story. It is a serialized work, in which each installment moves Kestrel Stoneheart a little farther along an adventurous road of discovery about herself and her world. I can't wait for you to join the journey!

CHAPTER ONE

Kestrel felt the beast's glare as a prickling at the nape of her neck. The long knife in her hand ceased its bloody work and she eased back on her heels, prepared to leap away from danger. Scarcely breathing, doing her best to ignore the sudden sweat slicking her skin, Kestrel lifted her head. Her gray eyes explored the dense pockets of brush and rocky gray outcrops littering the mountainside. She saw nothing out of the ordinary, but the hunted feeling remained.

The beast was lurking somewhere, working itself into a killing frenzy. She guessed it was growing weary of her taunting and would attack soon. No more stalking, no more playing. Only death. Hers.

"I cannot fight you here," she muttered, praying for the time she needed to reach the high mountain meadow she had chosen to make her stand.

Flipping her dark braid over her shoulder, Kestrel went back to gutting and skinning the last of the three rabbits she had snared the night before.

She paused every few seconds to scan the rocky slopes around her, but the beast remained hidden.

When she finished with the rabbit, she left the entrails where they lay—a grisly treat to further stoke the beast's hunger and, she admitted, another taunt. She tied the carcass beside the other two rabbits on her woven leather belt. Blood dribbled over one leg of her doeskin trousers, staining them with crimson scrawls that, by day's end, would darken to ugly brown. A shame to ruin the trousers, but it was a small sacrifice on the road to achieving her goal.

Tying a final knot, Kestrel remembered what her mother, Tessa, had said the last time they spoke. *Promise me you'll be safe, Kes.*

How can a Potential ever be truly safe? Kestrel had thought at the time, standing with Tessa on the porch of their cabin, the morning air cool and fragrant with pine sap and huckleberries an hour before the sun rose. With a straight face, she had made the promise her mother wanted to hear.

If Tessa could see how Kestrel had turned herself into a piece of walking bait, she would be horrified. But then, Tessa did not truly understand Kestrel's commitment to becoming a Red Hand of their tribe.

With a last wary glance around—nothing moved, save a jay swooping along the edge of the forest far below her vantage point—Kestrel stood and rubbed the soft leather soles of her boots through the pool of blood on the rock she had used as a butchering table. She had to delay the battle until she was ready to fight, but at the same time keep the beast interested. For that, only the smell of slaughter would do.

Choosing a path, Kestrel picked her way across a shifting tongue of gray-black rocks and boulders, which had been tumbling down from the jagged peaks soaring above her since long before the Red Fever ravaged the world and ushered in an age known as the Great Sorrow. The clouds massing above the crags had taken on an angry, bruised look. A storm was building. That could help her ... or make things much worse. She chose to believe the former.

After a few more miles, Kestrel slipped into the brush growing around the gnarled trunk of a lightning blasted pine. She paused to sip from her waterskin, and almost choked when she heard the rattle of stone nearby. Her gaze flicked over her back trail, upslope, then down. She saw nothing. Hopefully it stayed that way, at least for a little while longer.

She could have fought the beast anywhere besides the meadow, but as a Potential she'd had to disclose the battleground to the village Elders, who in turn might or might not have sent an observer. An observer was forbidden to intervene, even if it meant sparing the Potential from certain death. A Potential never knew for sure if anyone was watching them complete the rite of the Kill, and not knowing kept them honest. But even if Kestrel knew for sure that no one was scrutinizing her, she would still do all she could to reach the meadow, just as she had said she would. She wanted to become a Red Hand more than anything else in life, and that meant keeping her honor. Besides all the rest, the Ancestors were always near. They saw all, and were swift to curse liars.

Kestrel stood motionless, except for her fingers. They tapped restlessly against the handle of the hunting knife her father had presented to her before she departed the village. The weapon, which was longer than her forearm, had previously felt good hanging from her belt. Heavy, powerful, a deadly extension of her arm. As with choosing her place of battle, so too had she chosen her weapon—the same knife her father had once used to take off the head of a Stone Dog with a single, powerful blow.

She had believed the knife was lucky. Now, envisioning her hidden foe's golden eyes, long yellow teeth and deadly claws, the bit of sharp metal seemed as useless as a rotten stick.

She was about to step away from cover, but froze when a familiar worry assailed her. What if, despite all her best efforts, the beast had sensed her wariness and fled? Each Potential had only one chance to perform the rite of the Kill, and thus earn the right to stand beneath the Bone Tree and become a Red Hand, a warrior of her tribe. If a Potential failed, they were cast out from the village. The harsh rule ensured that only the most dedicated and skillful individuals risked becoming a Red Hand. For sixteen years, she had listened to the stories about those who failed, stories told by saddened villagers who gave failures a different name: *unworthy.*

"No," she murmured, eyes widening with dread. Those deemed unworthy made their way to the Dead Lands. As soon as they stepped foot across the scorched boundary, the air itself caught fire and melted the flesh from their bones. A terrible way to die, but dying, all the villagers agreed, was better than living in disgrace.

I don't want to die ... not like that, Kestrel thought, and drew the knife from its sheath. The blade was dull gray with dark pits along its length that spoke of its great age, but the edge shone like a thin band of quicksilver.

She touched the knife to her palm, hesitated, and then made a single, quick slash. A gasp of pain squeezed through her lips at the ancient steel's hungry bite, but the pain faded quickly, replaced by a feeling of power and strength surging through her.

She lifted her hand, fingers squeezed tight. A stream of blood dribbled from her fist to splatter over the foliage clawing at her legs and the rocks at her feet. The beast wanted *her* blood, not that of a few rabbits, and it was not alone in that desire.

In a low voice, she intoned, "I call upon the Ancestors of the House of the Red Hand to lend me your courage and cunning and strength. I call upon the Ancestors of the House of the Red Hand to deliver the beast into my hands."

A sharp gust swept down the mountains, hooting through hollows, scouring bare rocks with grit, tugging at her braid. The wind faded almost soon as begun, as if the Ancestors had spoken with the voice of the world. Had it been a real sign from her people's protectors, or only the approaching storm?

A sign. It must have been!

Kestrel slid the knife back into its sheath with a hand that shook with reverential awe, and then she hurried off along the faint game trail, following its upward, winding path through the fading shadows cast by the ragged line of peaks still laced with bands of last winter's snow. Higher still, thunderheads jostled together, growing darker.

Far behind her, concealed within the shadows of a dense thicket, a pair of hungry golden eyes marked her ascent.

CHAPTER TWO

After a few more hours of hard climbing, the day had grown old, and the sun had vanished behind the gathering clouds. The wind was stronger now, and the rich, damp scent of far off rain perfumed the air.

Kestrel struggled across another scree field, and leaped over an icy stream tumbling down its far edge. As the first rumble of thunder shook the world, she knelt to fill her waterskin. She gulped at the thin mountain air, her senses tingling, alert for any sign that the beast was still after her. When she glanced around, she saw nothing, but imagined she could feel its nearness and its caution.

The Ancestors were fickle at the best of times, but she believed with all her heart that they had accepted her blood sacrifice, and in so doing had filled the beast with an inescapable desire to devour her.

They must have! she thought, desperate to avoid the shame of failing. If she failed this final test, her father, Matthias, one of the village's six

Elders, would be slow to condemn her. As would her mother, who had an unrestrained and somewhat embarrassing love for her youngest child. Kestrel's brother, however, would not hesitate to mock her, and worse.

Aiden was only two years older than she was, but he had become a Red Hand when he was fourteen, and by the time he was her age, he had been raised to a warchief. No one in the village had ever earned that honor so young, and to Kestrel's mind, it had gone to her brother's head in the worst possible ways. But no matter what her family thought or felt, if she did not succeed, she would be dead to them, and to her people.

Pushing aside thoughts of failure, Kestrel scanned the boulder-strewn terrain falling away back the way she had come. She saw nothing close by, but farther off, down where the feet of the mountains spread out to become foothills covered in yellow grass and blue sage, she saw one of the nameless old cities. Its great towers of glass and steel glinted dully in the failing light, as if they still held the promise of life. If she squinted just so, she could almost imagine the city filled with people and bustling with activity. But that was just an illusion. It was a dead place, and forbidden, emptied of life by the Red Fever. Now, as told around Reaptime bonfires, the old cities were full of spirits that longed to steal away the warmth of the living. She would never go into such a place, and saw no reason to look at it. Besides, she had greater troubles closer to hand. The beast.

She searched her surroundings again, looking for any sign.

Her hopes had begun to drop, but then she noticed a patch of tawny fur within a tangle of brush upslope from her. Kestrel's heart sped up when, for just an instant, she caught sight of a hateful golden eye peering at her. In that moment, she felt the beast's desire to rip her limb from limb and strip the meat from her bones. Because she was the daughter of an Elder, Kestrel had chosen the most fearsome and cunning opponent imaginable. To do less, in hopes of gaining favor from her father's station in the village, would have brought shame to her and her family.

"Come for me, then," she whispered, smiling to herself. It was time to up the stakes.

Feigning an injury to her leg, she made a show of clambering up a series of stairlike granite slabs until coming to a steep ridge covered in grass, stunted fir trees, and a few scraggly aspens. She did not bother looking over her shoulder; she felt the beast closing. Still cautious, still hunting, but coming with more boldness than before.

After cresting the spine of the ridge, she dropped off the other side and slipped into a shadowed forest growing up the opposite slope. She was less than a mile from her destination.

Pointing her face into the gusty breath of the coming storm, Kestrel continued upward, every few steps rubbing her bloody hand over the rough bark of tree trunks and through the needles of low hanging limbs. The blood of the rabbits had dried on her trousers, and the skinned carcasses now looked leathery, but the smell of raw meat still wafted from them. She meant them for her victory dinner.

Occasional peeks over her shoulder revealed that the beast was becoming more audacious. It had closed the distance to less than a hundred strides. Ghostlike, it stole from one tree to the next, one bush to another, and the wind was doing its job of carrying the scent of her blood and that of the rabbits to the beast's flaring nostrils.

Kestrel uttered a pitiful bleating sound, mimicking the cry of a wounded animal, and increased her pace until she was just short of running. It was hard work faking a limp at such speed, but her confidence was soaring.

Wind gusts thrashed the trees, and carried the booming peals of thunder across the ridgeline. The steep trail soon flattened and became a wide, forested bench.

Without slowing, still offering up occasional squeals to lure the beast, Kestrel leaped fallen logs and crashed through thickets of brush. Branches slapped and clawed at her face, drawing raw lines across her cheeks and brow. Roots and rocks threatened to upset her footing with every step. Despite the wind and thunder, Kestrel could hear the beast's huffing growls closing in.

Breath ripping at her lungs, Kestrel flew over the carpet of rock-studded pine straw, but a heaviness was beginning to sink into her legs. She had not fully accounted for the thinness of the air so high, and was running out of strength. If she did not reach the meadow soon, she would have no choice but to turn and fight. She did not want to do that—to remain true to her purpose, she *could not* do that—but neither did she want to be eaten alive.

Fighting through the exhaustion, she struggled on, climbing like a squirrel up and over a jumble of granite boulders, down the other side, and back into thick stands of pine.

Brush crashed behind her, and rapidly nearing snarls stitched her pounding heart with threads of fear. She searched for landmarks, but the forest flashing by her had become a gray-green blur. *Where is the meadow?*

A rock rolled underfoot and she pitched violently forward. She tucked her shoulder to roll, but the angle of her flight was wrong. The top of her head crashed against the ground, her neck cracked, and she flipped over onto her back hard enough to knock what little breath she had from her chest.

When Kestrel rolled to her belly, she found that her jarring flight had brought her to the brushy edge of the meadow—her chosen battleground. She tried to push herself up, but her body felt as though it weighed ten times as much as normal.

A soft drumming sensation moved up through the ground and into her hands. She shot a frantic look back the way she had come. The murderous beast was bearing down on her in great, leaping bounds, its tail a flailing whip streaming out behind it.

She slashed her bloody hand through the grass and dried leaves, came up with a fist-sized rock, and hurled it at the creature's rounded head. A dull, cracking thud and a yowling snarl told her that her aim had been true, but she did not see the blow. She was already on her feet and tearing across the meadow.

Her unexpected attack had given the beast pause, but only for a moment. She had not run ten strides before she heard it take up the chase again.

Fear exploded into rampaging panic inside her chest. In one shameful instant, she wondered what demented fool had decided that the rite of the Kill should qualify someone to become a Red Hand.

She shoved that disgraceful idea from her mind, yet the stain of it remained. The only way to cleanse herself of the momentary weakness was to face her fear, and that meant fighting to the death.

A second before she found herself tumbling through the air once more, she heard the rip of leather and felt a row of burning stripes blossom across her calf.

This time, she had no chance to attempt a graceful landing. Nearly upside down, she landed on her face and slid through a cluster of spiny wildflowers, arms spread wide, legs curling up over her back in a flailing arc. The beast slammed into Kestrel's belly and sent her cartwheeling.

Kestrel scrambled to her feet, her mouth gaping wide to draw a breath that would not come, her knife held out before her in a desperate bid to keep the beast at a safe distance.

Having no fear of sharp steel, her enemy pounced.

Claws flashed by her cheek and shredded the shoulder of her doeskin shirt. Several more fiery stripes took root there, but she barely felt them. Kestrel spread her shaking legs for balance, and thrust her hand against the soft fur of creature's neck. At the same time, she buried her knife in the beast's flank. It twisted and screamed, its pistoning back legs driving its weight against her. She stabbed again, and in answer, the beast raked its claws across her hip.

The breath she had wanted finally came, but just as quickly burst out of her in an agonized cry. She made one more frantic stab, but the blade skittered across the beast's ribs. Her counterattack was enough to break their lumbering embrace.

Kestrel reeled backward, her eyes fixed on the beast crouched off to one side, its jaws spread to reveal teeth that gleamed like weathered gold. When the beast took a cautious step backward, as if reconsidering its prey, she did the only thing that might change its mind. She ran.

CHAPTER THREE

Kestrel sprinted a hundred strides farther into the meadow, before accepting that she could go no farther at that pace if she wanted a chance of winning the coming fight.

She spun and walked backwards, expecting to see the beast explode out of the high grass and race toward her, but it was gone. The bite of her knife had given it something to think about, to be sure, but there had been fury and hate lighting its eyes, and she knew it would not give up.

Hesitantly, she touched her savaged shoulder. Her fingers came away greasy with blood. Further searching revealed four bloody tears in the hip of her snug trousers, and another raw foursome along her calf—the blood from that wound had soaked her boot. Trousers could be mended, but the rips in her flesh were another matter. She was bleeding heavily, and already felt lightheaded. Even if she managed to staunch the flow, such wounds were prone to flesh-rot, even under the best circumstances. But these were hardly the best circumstances. She was a long way from home, where her mother kept a cupboard stocked with healing herbs and tonics. Gathering those same herbs anytime soon was unlikely, and to brew tonics, which took a mind more skilled in those arts than hers, was out of the question.

Kestrel cast a longing glance at the pond off to one side, but resisted the urge to go cleanse her injuries. There would be time for that later. *Maybe.*

Seeing no reason to go any farther, Kestrel halted, knife steady in her hand, but swaying on her feet. There was still no sign of the beast. Wind shrieked down off the mountain slopes, now carrying with it occasional spatters of rain. Black-bellied clouds, crawling with tentacles of blue-white fire, pushed over the peaks.

She did not want to die here. *I cannot fail. I cannot!*

With that desperate thought blaring in her mind, she spun in a tight circle, searching, knife held low to stab an enemy that remained hidden ... or gone.

Do I chase after it, run it down and force it to fight?

The idea took root while she gazed toward the edge of the forest. Whatever decision she might have come to was stolen away when the beast oozed like smoke from a cluster of saplings growing together thick as dog hair. Blood flecked its muzzle, and more flowed from its billowing ribs. As it drew nearer, she heard the deep, wet gurgle of its breathing. She had wounded it terribly, perhaps mortally, but it was far from dead.

And neither am I, she thought, ignoring the queasy faintness she felt from her blood loss.

The beast came closer, taking its time, an eerie, hateful light smoldering deep in its golden eyes. Its black-tipped tail lashed back and forth, indifferent to the storm's powerful gusts.

A tickle of uncertainty pebbled Kestrel's skin in gooseflesh. She had chosen to fight this animal for its lethal tenacity, and she had enticed it further with blood. Perhaps she should have stuck to the tactics of the bird of her namesake, and set an ambush?

She shook her head, refusing to second-guess herself. It was too late for that, and far too late to turn back.

The beast padded closer, muscles bunching in its powerful haunches. Lightning flashed, and its eyes seemed to catch fire for a moment, before going a dark gold again.

Then the creature stopped no more than ten feet away. There was cunning in its stare. Too much cunning.

"What are you waiting for?" Kestrel demanded, her voice shrill.

Its shoulders rippled as it fell into a crouch.

Kestrel mimicked the creature's stance,

bending her knees, spreading her feet and arms. She slashed her knife between them.

With a growling hiss, the beast laid its ears flat against its skull. Kestrel tried her own growl, but it sounded more like a whimper.

The beast's tongue, streaked with blood, lolled through the ragged gate formed by its teeth. No matter how insane it sounded, Kestrel thought sure the creature was laughing at her. That made her more afraid, but also angry.

"I will not die today!" Kestrel cried, and charged ahead at the same instant the beast leaped.

They met in a squalling tangle, her knife slashing, and its claws tearing. Rending red agony ripped across her belly. Screaming, she sank the blade into the creature's flank, once and again. Dirty yellow teeth snapped together an inch from her nose, then yawned wide again for a bite that would pierce her skull.

Kestrel reared back, and the beast's greater weight put her off balance. As she fell, she lashed out. The blade sank to the hilt. She clung to the knife's handle, letting her weight drag the sharp edge downward, tearing open the creature's side, ripping a great bloody gash in its belly. It yowled and twisted away, leaving her behind.

Kestrel sprawled on her back, stupid with weakness and terror, lines of fire spreading from her newest wounds. More than any presence of mind, instinct commanded her to roll to her side.

The beast was circling, trailing its entrails behind it. It favored one foreleg, and was dragging the opposite rear leg. Yet its golden eyes still burned with killing hate.

Kestrel could not breathe, and her limbs trembled. Blood ran into one eye, turning half the world red.

Get up! she ordered herself. *Get up and fight! For your Ancestors, and for the House of the Red Hand, get up!*

The beast circled closer, its movements shaky. A ceaseless growl rumbled from its throat, a sound of rage and fear, something she fully understood.

The beast charged, and to Kestrel's eyes, it seemed to be moving as if through cold honey. She surged to her feet. Just before they clashed again, she tripped over a stone, and barely missed having a claw-tipped paw tear off her head.

Stumbling forward, she rammed her blade deep into the center of the beast's chest. There was a breathless quality to its pained scream.

They fell together and rolled. Kestrel drew out her knife and plunged it again, and once more. The creature spit and snarled, its body shuddering. Twisting hard, she came up on top, blade poised to strike, but not falling.

The beast, her Kill, was dead.

CHAPTER FOUR

Caught in a haze of pain, Kestrel stared down at the beast. Death had softened its fury, stolen its murderous intent. It was no longer a monster that stalked nightmares, but a lion. In death, she could appreciate the grace and majesty she had stolen from it. The elation she had always dreamed she would feel at this moment was nowhere to be found. In its place, she felt pity, even regret.

"You fought fair and well," she murmured, running her fingers through its fur. "Today you made me a warrior of my tribe. I thank you for your sacrifice ... and I'm sorry I made you pay it."

Bowing her head, she let silent tears flow. They were a meager payment for the life she had taken, but she had nothing else to give.

When the first drops of rain began to fall, she wiped her eyes and explored the lacerations on her belly. The new wounds were not deep, but they needed tending.

Using her knife she cut the sleeves off her shirt. The shredded doeskin rags made poor bandages, but they would serve. After making several long strips, she bound the wounds. With that done, she turned back to the lion.

While her injuries were more than enough to prove she had been in a fight, to stand before her people at the Bone Tree ceremony, where she would formally become a Red Hand, she needed the lion's head and hide to prove what she had fought. But for now, she was still a hunter, so she would make a pack from the lion's hide to carry its meat.

Weak as she was, the thought of carrying such a burden made her legs shake, but all within her tribe despised weakness as much as she did, so she set to work.

She had skinned her first deer when six years old, and now, ten years later, she had much more experience. Using sure strokes, she quickly parted the lion's skin from its belly to its neck, then began alternately cutting and peeling the hide off its body like a coat. She laid the hide fur-side down, rolling the carcass as she worked, careful to keep it out of the dirt. Normally she would have used a ground cloth, but when a Potential set out for the Kill, they carried only their clothes and the weapon of their choosing.

She carefully cut off the lion's head and set it aside. Stray hairs clung to her bloody hands and the knife blade so thickly that even the drumming rain could not clean off the mess. There was no helping it. She would not have a chance to bathe for a while.

Kestrel placed a knife between the hollow of the lion's flank and the swell of its haunch, and prepared to make the first cut into its meat.

A flicker of movement drew her eyes.

Barely turning her head, she looked to the rocky slopes rising high above the meadow, and saw a group of men picking their way down the slope. She held still, not wanting to catch their attention, as they had caught hers.

The rain began falling harder, blanketing the world in a gray shroud. Lightning flared sporadically. Thunder rolled. Through the stuttering, murky haze, she counted at least eight figures dressed in leather and fur. A few held bows, the rest carried spears. Like her, they would also have long knives. *But who are they?* she wondered, her sight hampered by the pounding rain.

Kestrel held no hope that the newcomers were people she knew—if there was an observer about, they would never show themselves. That left members of another tribe. And, as they were obviously willing to break their treaty by encroaching on the hunting grounds of her people, that marked them as enemies.

Tall Ones? An icy prickle snaked its way down her spine. She tried to swallow, but her throat was too dry. The Tall Ones lived far to the north. Kestrel had never seen one, and did not know anyone who had, but she had heard the stories of those vile folk, they who were given to strange rituals that lit the night sky behind the walls of their village for miles around. As far as she knew, no Tall One had ever ventured so far from their territory, and no one dared attack them, for fear of having their souls stolen, or worse.

So if not the Tall Ones, then she was looking at either Stone Dogs or Black Ears. Both tribes were great enemies of her people, and it appeared that one tribe or the other had sent out a raiding party. It was just a matter of time before they saw her. Only the forest offered any protection and hope of escape.

Kestrel cast about, her heart thudding as hard as it had when she faced the lion. She was tempted to leave behind its skin and head, but if she failed to return to the village with proof of the Kill, then all she had gone through would have been for nothing. Not only that, without proof, she would be sent into the Dead Lands. The meat, however, would have to remain behind. There was no time to butcher the carcass, and there was no chance she could escape while carrying a burden that weighed at least half as much as she did.

"I'm sorry," she said again to the lion, bundling the beast's head into its hide.

Still on her knees, she waited until another flash of lightning ripped across the sky, hoping the flare would momentarily blind her enemies. When the thunder rolled over her, she lurched to her feet and made for the woods as fast as her feet would carry her.

She had not crossed half the distance when a chorus of shouts rose far behind her.

Kestrel did not bother looking over her shoulder. There was no doubt her enemies were coming. Sucking wind, she quickened her pace through the tall meadow grass, her feet slipping in fresh mud. The forest seemed to recede from her. She ducked her head and ran faster. Reaching the thick cover of trees was her only hope.

Kestrel flinched when an arrow whistled past her ear and stabbed into the ground twenty strides ahead, but she did not slow. Crashing through a bush, her feet became tangled, and the bundle almost flew from her grasp. Stumbling, gasping, willing her feet and legs to stay strong, she righted herself and raced on.

The forest was fifty strides away ... now forty ... now thirty.

Another arrow tugged at her flapping braid. She barely noticed. The tree line was now no more than ten strides away. More arrows shrieked past her. One cut a tiny, burning notch out of her earlobe.

The forest was so close now.

Ten feet ... five feet.

Kestrel had no chance to veer away from the

tall, shadowed figure of a man who stepped out from behind the nearest tree. He raised something in his hand, she heard a sharp popping sound, felt a piercing sting in her shoulder. Running at full speed, she bowled him over, took a few more graceless, lurching strides, and flipped over a fallen log.

From somewhere behind her, she heard a groggy curse, but could not see the man she had knocked aside. Better if their collision had broken his neck. That it had not meant she had one more enemy to deal with. Nine against one.

Strangling a cry of frustration, she snatched up her bundle and ran deeper into the forest.

CHAPTER FIVE

Rain dripped from above, but the thickly twined pine boughs kept off most of the deluge and served as a windbreak. Their tight weave also blocked out most of the weak gray daylight, making it harder to see.

Each shambling step Kestrel took left her weaker, and her panting breaths failed to fill her lungs. Dark spots haunted her vision, and more than once she found herself listing to the side, an instant from falling over. Terror twisted like a snake inside her. She could not go on much longer without rest. All the blood she had lost after battling the lion had left her weak, and she was getting weaker by the minute.

If I stop, the Stone Dogs, or the Black Ears, or whoever they are, will take me prisoner. The thought sent a shudder through her.

Her people abhorred taking prisoners, but her mentor, One-Ear Tom, often told of the horrendous treatment Stone Dogs and Black Ears inflicted upon their captives—most did not survive more than a few days. Those who did, and managed to escape, were never the same.

Another shudder rippled her body when she thought of Old Regar's weeping eye socket, and the crisscrossing scars lining his face. A raiding party of Black Ears had caught him when he had been Young Regar, a promising Red Hand. They had done things to him that no one talked about, and those torments had turned him from a strong warrior into a fearful man who screamed and wet himself at the sight of fire or blades.

Not wanting to turn out like Old Regar, Kestrel forced herself to keep putting one foot in front of the other.

A brief flurry of shouts filtered through the forest behind her. They sounded distant, eager, angry. She concentrated on her path.

In order to keep within the forest, she needed to stay on the north side of the ridgeline she had climbed earlier, which lay somewhere off to her right. She picked out the weathered gray hulk of a dead snag off to her left. It stood out like a ghost amid the living trees, and keeping it in sight was easy. Better yet, she was now moving downhill.

She kept going until the shouts faded to nothing. After plunging through a wide huckleberry patch, Kestrel risked pausing long enough to catch her breath. It was not enough to ease the weakness in her legs, or to clear the gauzy blotches of darkness pressing in at the edges of her vision, so she sat down and scooted up under a nest of tangled roots jutting off the stump of a fallen tree. Resting was dangerous, but for now, she could go no farther.

Craning her neck, she glanced back the way she had come. The forest was alive with motion, but as far as she could tell, it was only tree branches rustling in the wind. Not trusting her eyes, she cocked her head and opened her mouth slightly, a posture that often helped her to hear better. The only noise was the deep, hollow whooshing and rattle of the storm blowing through the forest, and the crazed drumming of rain. *Did they lose my trail, or give up?*

The apparent good fortune made her uneasy. She had not run all that far, and not very fast at that. There was no way her enemies had given up. And if they had lost her trail, they would find it again soon enough.

She knew she needed to get up, but hidden as she was within the tree roots felt safer than running blindly through the forest. *Just a few more moments, then I'll go.*

Breathing easier now, Kestrel let her head droop, and felt something sharp jab her chin. With a curious frown, she felt around and found something stuck in her shoulder. She pulled the object free with a hiss, and held up a shining metal tube with a stubby spike on one end, and springing fins on the other, like the fletching of an arrow. *A dart? How—*

The thought cut off when she remembered the man she had run over at the edge of the forest, and the popping sound she had heard when he pointed his weapon at her. She tossed the dart away with a scornful curse. If her enemies thought a child's toy could stop her, they were sorely mistaken.

Kestrel looked off in the direction she needed to go. If she kept going downhill, there was a creek in the bottom of the ravine that ran for perhaps ten miles, maybe a little a farther, before feeding the river that flowed near her village. If her enemies followed her that far, she could always jump into the river and let it carry her most of the way home. Swimming would be hard while holding onto her bundle, but that was better than running and hiding in the mountains. The way she felt right now, her body so heavy, there would be no running at all....

Her eyes flared open at a crash of thunder. She gazed about, stunned to see that the puny light of day had grown darker than ever. She lifted her hand to wipe her face, and froze. Despite the cover the gnarled roots provided, she was soaked to the skin, as was the lion skin nestled in her lap. The only thing warm on her was the blood seeping from under her makeshift bandages. There was an ache in her knees, and her feet were all pins and needles. She had blacked out. One moment she had been awake, just resting a moment, and the next she had drifted away.

Kestrel peered about, and the forest appeared empty. She tried to jump to her feet, but instead fell flat on her face. Cramps knotted the muscles in her legs, her belly, and her back. The slashes made by the lion's claws burned like trenches filled with hot coals.

Teeth gritted against a scream of agony, Kestrel kneaded her legs until she was able to straighten them. Once she felt better, if not stronger, she caught hold of a dripping root and hoisted herself up. The lumpy bulk of the lion skin lay nearby, but before she could take it in hand, the snap of a tree branch whipped her head around.

Twenty strides away, she made out the hunched shadow of a man creeping through the forest. Crackling lightning lit the sky, and in that brief flash, she saw his tangled black hair, and a long scruffy beard hanging from his chin. He held a spear, its tip as long as her knife.

Darkness fell again, thunder rolled.

She blinked a few times, clearing the afterimages. Although he was harder to see than before, she could still make out the way he was turning his head one way, then the other. If he had found her trail, he would have been on her already. As close as he was, she could not hope to remain hidden for long.

Kestrel stood stock still, taking shallow breaths,

until he passed behind a cluster of saplings. Only then did she hunker down, careful to move slowly, despite the way her flexing muscles pulled at her injuries. She glanced at the bundled lion skin again. For the second time, she considered leaving it behind. And for the second time, she decided against it.

She had just picked up the sopping bundle of bloody fur, when two voices rose up at once. "There she is!" and "Found her!" followed by the crash of men surging through the forest.

Kestrel forgot the weakness in her limbs, the utter exhaustion cloaking her mind and, like a deer set upon by wild dogs, she fled.

CHAPTER SIX

Shouts of victory filled the dark forest, seeming to double, then triple, until Kestrel feared there were not eight or nine men after her, but an entire raiding party. And they were closing fast.

Kestrel stumbled through the dark, dodging this way and that each time an obstacle loomed before her. She leaped a log here, ducked a branch there, always one step from sprawling on her face. Hot, shuddering gasps tore at her lungs like broken glass. Her injuries screamed within her flesh, their voices sharp and fiery. Hope of any sort had soared out of her grasp.

Her mother's voice rose up in the back of her mind. *There are times when you must become the rabbit.* Kestrel had considered that advice the word of a coward. Until now.

But if she was to play the rabbit, she would do so with a weapon in hand. Shifting the sodden hide to the crook of her arm, she drew her long knife.

A stutter of lightning brightened the forest, and she saw that she was nearly to the ghost snag that she had marked out before. Another flickering blast of lightning revealed men bounding along beside her, angling toward her, their spears waving. When a hulking man veered in from the side and blocked her path, Kestrel lifted her knife and locked her elbow, turning her arm into a spear. A second later she collided with him and bounced away.

Kestrel rolled through a soaking bed of ferns and slammed against a tree trunk. The knife was no longer in her hand, and the man, lost to sight but somewhere near, was making horrid, breathless gagging noises.

Still holding the bundle, Kestrel lunged to her feet and tore away into the night. The way was getting steeper, making it harder to stay upright. She thrashed one hand for balance, while holding tight to the bundle with the other.

Kestrel never saw the drop off.

One moment she was running toward the gray snag, her feet pounding the ground, the next she was soaring like a startled bird through the rain-lashed air. She hit hard, and her breath exploded from her chest. Then she was rolling and sliding along at a stunning, jarring pace. She banged against the base of the snag, bounced off like a rawhide ball, and skidded to a stop a little farther down the rocky slope. A crackling groan sounded above her, followed by a hollow whoosh, and then the top of the ghost snag smashed down beside her, spraying her with chunks of dry-rotted wood and choking her with a cloud of itchy dust. If it had fallen two feet closer, it would have crushed her like a bug.

On the slope of above her, shadows of men were gathering together and shouting their triumph.

You have to get up. You have to run. Kestrel knew these things, but she could not get her limbs to work.

Her foes spilt up and began making their way down toward her, leaping over boulders and fallen trees. She had seconds before they were upon her.

When rough fingers caught hold of her shoulder and dug savagely into the gouges there, Kestrel's thoughts ceased. Shrieking like a demon, she clamped both hands around the arm dragging her up off the ground, twisted her head around, and sank her teeth into her captor's wrist.

"Damn it all, Kes! Stop that!" The voice was as rough as the hand that held her, but she knew it well.

"Aiden? Why are *you* here?"

"Get to the stream," her brother ordered, his flat voice eerily calm.

Kestrel feared a nightmare had caught her in its clutches. None of this made sense. Aiden could not be here. "W-what?" she stammered.

Once Aiden had her on her feet, he shoved her away, and moved a few steps up the slope. The men who had pursued her were still clambering near, oblivious of the newcomer.

Maybe they don't see him, Kestrel thought, *because he isn't really here.*

"Go, Kes. *Now!*" The last word came out as an uncompromising roar, shattering her bewilderment.

The men scrambling down the mountainside skidded to a stop as one. Kestrel backed away, her eyes wide, even as her brother moved forward. He was no longer paying attention to her.

"Who's that?" one of the men asked.

Aiden did not answer. Lightning flashed, and she saw her brother holding a knife in each hand, each nearly a foot longer than the one she had lost.

"Two young Red Hands, is my guess," said another man, chuckling as if at a fine joke.

"Our lucky day."

"No need to fear," another voice called, sounding reasonable. "We come as friends."

Kestrel almost laughed at such a ludicrous idea, but even if she had, no one would have heard it, for her brother was already moving, his blades flashing dully in the night.

Two men had fallen dead, and a third had dropped his spear to clutch at the slithering skein of intestines pouring from his severed belly, before the others could react. By then, Aiden had settled deep within their broken line, roaring and killing. The survivors slashed the air where Aiden had been with their spears. He spun through them, a whirlwind of death.

Steel rang against wood and flesh and bone.

Another man went down, the blood spraying from his neck blacker than the night. Another followed, the stump of his arm spurting, and a gut-wrenching gurgling sound bursting from his throat.

Kestrel backed away from the furious fight, but more she retreated from her brother's rage. It was not the first time she had seen him furious, but she had never seen his wrath displayed so openly.

Another man fell amongst his writhing companions, but he lay as unmoving as the dead wood littering the stony ground.

The last man held his spear out before him to block another attack. "There's no need for this! I'm your friend!" he cried, as if he really believed the lie. Lightning painted his terror-stretched features silver and black.

In that brief light, Kestrel also saw Aiden, his clean-shaved face spattered and running with crimson gore, his pale eyes burning with the same eerie fire that had lit the lion's eyes.

When darkness fell again, she saw only blurs of movement. Steel sang a high shrill note, wood crunched, and the last man loosed a frightened screech. When the steel sang again, his last shout echoed away into the storm.

Only seven, Kestrel thought, counting the dead.

There had been eight coming down the mountain, and another at the edge of the forest.

"There are others!" she blurted, looking wildly about in the dark.

Her brother's silhouette turned slowly, his dripping blades held out to either side. "Why are you still here?" His voice was cold, uncompromising.

"There are more," she insisted.

"I'll worry about them. Now go, as I commanded you."

"I must find the lion skin," Kestrel murmured. "I need it to ... to prove my Kill." After seeing what Aiden had done, her achievement seemed trivial. Worse still, if he was here, then that meant he was the observer and....

And he helped me, she thought, sick with understanding. Aiden, who had never believed she should become a Red Hand, who had done all he could to discourage her, would never allow her to stand beneath the Bone Tree, and he would make no argument to keep her from being sent into the Dead Lands.

Aiden's broad-shouldered shape did not move and did not speak.

Numb of body and mind, Kestrel began a hasty search for the bundle. It made no sense to do so, with the way things had turned out, but she could not stop herself. Some part of her simply refused to accept that all her efforts had been wasted.

With her brother staring at her, judging her as he always did, her fingers were clumsy, and it seemed to take forever. Eventually she found the sodden hide up under a bush farther down the slope. The skull had fallen out, and she had to wrap it all up again.

As she stood up, she thought about her lost knife, but Aiden had already donned his knapsack and was making his way down into the black throat of the ravine. He had turned his back on her, as would her tribe when he told what had happened on the mountain.

Not knowing what else to do, feeling more lost and discouraged about her life and future than she could ever remember, she followed him.

CHAPTER SEVEN

Tripping and sliding down the steep ravine, soaked to the skin from the drumming rain, Kestrel struggled through the stormy darkness to keep up with her brother.

Now that the threat of becoming a prisoner was no longer spurring her on, the debilitating weakness of blood loss had once more settled into her limbs. Worse than that was Aiden's presence.

She wanted to believe she was on her way home to become a Red Hand, but Aiden had shown up and ruined everything by slaughtering the men who had chased her. Observers were not supposed to help Potentials, yet he had done so. He despised her, and always had, so she could find no reason that would have compelled him to give her aid ... unless his only purpose had been to shatter her dream.

A violent shiver rattled Kestrel's teeth and shook away her unsettling thoughts. She had been caught in the rain plenty of times while hunting, and knew what it was to be cold, even in the middle of summer, but the chill she felt now was closer to the bone-breaking frigidness felt on the frostiest nights of winter.

Only the deep lacerations she had taken from the lion's claws held any warmth at all—across her belly, her hip and shoulder, and more on her calf—but that warmth was a sharp, cruel heat that promised the looming sickness of flesh-rot.

The night seemed to go on forever. As she hobbled along after Aiden, feeling sick and dizzy, she forced her sluggish mind to reconsider the idea of being cast from the village and cursed to seek solace, brief as it would be, in the Dead Lands. Was her chance to become a Red Hand *really* gone? Aiden had helped her, it was true, but he had not helped with the Kill—that seemed crucial to her—and she had no intention of letting him help her get home. That she was following him meant nothing and broke no rules. They were just two people taking the same path to the same place. The final judgment, of course, rested with the Elders. It gave her a little hope.

She held the bundled lion skin wrapped tight around the beast's head to her chest with shaking hands. She licked rainwater off her lips to wet her parched tongue, but that only made her thirstier. Her waterskin hung at her elbow, but she did not have the strength to lift it.

Up ahead, Aiden said something over his

shoulder.

"What?" Kestrel croaked. It seemed impossible that only a few short hours ago she had been running up a ridgeline, tempting the lion to chase her to its doom.

Aiden halted and spoke again.

To Kestrel, it sounded as if he were underwater. Too weak to slow herself, she tottered forward. As she came closer to him, he seemed to fragment and puff apart. She tried to stop but could not. Her knees came unhinged, and then she was floating forward into blackness.

CHAPTER EIGHT

When Kestrel opened her eyes, she felt warm, despite the chill gray light of dawn just beginning to seep through the pines towering above her. The storm had passed, but it would be an hour or more before daylight revealed if the day would be fair or overcast. Being late summer, she guessed the former. It would be a month or more before the frosty mornings around Reaptime began to signal the nearness of coming winter.

She heard a gurgling stream off to one side, and to the other she saw the fitful light of a fire. The smell of roasting meat filled her nostrils, and she turned her head to find Aiden sitting cross-legged on the far side of the blaze, using his teeth to tear charred flesh off a bone.

"What happened?" she asked, her throat raw, hoarse. Other than that, she felt better than she had the previous night—not much better, but she would take what the Ancestors gave her. She raised her head a little, noting that he had cooked the rabbits she snared the day before—those she had used to tempt the lion to chase her up the mountain.

Aiden tossed the bone in the fire and watched it turn black, before raising his eyes. They were gray like hers, and empty of all but a familiar glimmer of scorn. "You fainted."

"I didn't!"

"Is there another name for falling on your face?"

As often happened when he criticized her, her tongue froze as hard as her brain. Eventually everything would thaw, and she would find an appropriate answer, hours or days later, but by then it would be too late.

Shame and anger warred inside her. She hated that he alone could make her feel so useless, foolish, and … *unworthy*. She hated more, especially right now, that she still loved him. Not just because he was her brother, but also because he was the perfect example of a Red Hand, and all that she had worked so hard to become.

She struggled to sit up. "The lion fought well, but I defeated it. After the Bone Tree ceremony, I'll be named a Red Hand." Still unsure if that day would ever come, she did not say it with as much confidence as she intended.

Aiden snorted and shook his shaved head. "You call that a victory?" he said, gesturing at her bandages and clothes. It was then that she noticed he had re-bandaged her wounds and applied

46

poultices filled with healing herbs. Splatters of mud, pine needles, and old blood covered the rest of her. Aiden added, "You look like a mountain fell on you."

"I fought with only a knife," she reminded him.

"Is that a boast, or an excuse for almost getting yourself killed?" He went on, raising his voice over hers when she tried to protest. "Many Potentials have fought lions with knives. Others have fought wolves, and even bears."

"And many have died in the attempt."

"Those who died were weak. Losing the weak makes the tribe stronger." Firelight played across Aiden's angular features, danced in his flat stare. Most backed down from that expression. Only their father did not. If she had not grown up with Aiden, she might have backed down herself. Still, it took all of her courage to hold her ground.

"What if those who died weren't weak or foolish, but just unlucky?"

Aiden leaned closer. "And what if you were just lucky?"

Kestrel felt her cheeks redden. How could she deny the question? She remembered all too well how she had stumbled the last time she and the lion clashed. If she had not, the beast would have ripped her head off with a powerful swipe of its claws. If that was not luck, then what was?

Aiden sat back, a smirk twisting his lips at the sight of her doubt and confusion. "Don't worry, little sister, I won't tell anyone what I saw in that meadow."

Kestrel's heart sped up a little. If he did not intend to tell what he had seen, then maybe he would not tell that he had helped her.

After a moment, she asked, "Why were you there at all?"

"I was your observer."

"But why you? Why not One-Ear Tom, or another Red Hand?"

Aiden shrugged. "You know how Mother is. She didn't want anything to happen to you. Neither did Father or One-Ear Tom. I volunteered because I guessed their worry was well founded. Turns out my suspicions were right. If you hadn't stumbled there at the end, that lion would even now be crunching on your bones."

A frown pinched Kestrel's brow. "And why did you let those warriors chase me for so long?"

He laughed. "I actually found myself hoping you'd fight them off on your own, and prove yourself worthy to be a Red Hand—they were just a mangy pack of Stone Dogs, after all. But you didn't fight them. You ran, as I thought you would. Lucky for you, I stayed around."

"Why *did* you stay?" she asked, unable to say what she really thought, that she wished he had gone away. Or better yet, had never come at all. The only thing that tempered the idea was that if he had not shown up, she would be a captive, or dead.

He sneered at her. "Because in my heart I knew you didn't have it in you to fight them off, and would need me to save you."

Kestrel's mouth fell open.

"Don't look so surprised, little sister. You've always been weak, and I've always known it. Father sees it, but refuses to believe what his eyes tell him. And Mother ... well, as much as I love her, I have no doubt you get your weakness from her."

"Just because she chose to be a farmer, and not a Red Hand, does not make her weak," Kestrel said in Tessa's defense. "And I'm not weak." She wished that were not so true at the moment. Just sitting up and talking had left her so exhausted that she wanted to lie back down. "I can carry as much as most men."

"No, you cannot. But I don't mean the strength of your arms. You are weak here and here," Aiden said, tapping his chest, then the side of his head. "Instead of celebrating over your Kill, I saw you weep. Do you think one of those Stone Dogs up the ravine would have wept at cutting out your heart? Black Ears are even worse. They would have laughed as they chopped you to pieces, but only after they had their way with you for a few days—or *months*."

Kestrel had no answer. She knew what Aiden said about Stone Dogs and Black Ears was true. She also knew he was judging her too harshly. He seemed to think that because he was the youngest Red Hand ever, and in turn the youngest ever warchief, that he could dole out wise criticism with the voice of an elder—no one doubted he would become a leader of the tribe one day, but so far, that day had not come.

As for the lion, she could admit that she had felt compassion for the beast, but was that so wrong, when it had fought for its life with all the strength and determination that she had? Her weeping had been her meager way to pay the creature the respect it had earned. Before she could figure out a way to explain what filled her heart, Aiden spoke up again.

"The day will come when your luck runs out, little sister, when no one is around to save you. When that day comes, one of our enemies will take your blood or your body. That's when you will understand that it would've been better if I told the truth about how you *really* beat the lion."

"If you think so," Kestrel snapped, "then why not tell the Elders when we return?" If she were not so tired and hurt, she would have leaped across the fire and kicked her brother in the teeth. At least, that was what she wished she could do.

"If you really have honor enough to become Red Hand, then you will tell them yourself—but I know you won't. As it stands, I can afford to let you fail on your own."

Kestrel felt the sting of tears in her eyes. She blinked them away, and hoped it was not obvious. "I have honor and strength," she said, just above a whisper.

"You don't, Kes. Not even a little. But I don't need to tell our people what they will learn soon enough."

"What does that mean?"

He lifted a leather cord from the neck of his shirt. Four human teeth hung from it. His Kill had been a Black Ear, another living man, the most dangerous of prey. Aiden was the first in many generations to pit himself against such a Kill.

"Once you hang the bones of your Kill around your neck," he said, "you'll be counted as a Red Hand. And if there's one thing all Red Hands are expected to do, it is to fight our enemies. When your first battle comes, and you begin weeping and shaking like you did over that lion, everyone will know you are not a true Red Hand, and never were—that's if you even survive your first battle." He looked at her, lips wrinkled in disgust, as if he did not care if she died or not. "On that day, you will remember this moment, and you'll wish the lion had ended you."

Does he really hate me so much? The answer, it seemed, was self-evident. "You're wrong," she whispered.

Aiden dismissed her protest with a wave of his

hand. "You need food for strength," he said, flinging half of a roasted rabbit into her lap. "Friends of those men I killed might come looking for us. If so, I don't want to have to fight them off *and* carry you at the same time."

Kestrel inhaled sharply. "There were others besides the seven you killed! Eight on the mountain, and another at the edge of the forest. I knocked him over."

Aiden rolled his eyes. "I never saw them. The first likely ran for his life, and the second was probably a bush you mistook for a man."

Kestrel ground her teeth together. "I *saw* him!"

"What did he look like?"

Kestrel shook her head uncertainly. "I ... I don't know. Everything was happening so fast."

"Like I said, you ran into a bush."

"No!" Kestrel shouted, meaning to tell about the dart the man at the edge of the forest had shot her with, but Aiden cut her off.

"Believe me, Kes, if there were any others around, I would have killed them. Now, eat."

"But—"

"*Eat!*"

The last of her resistance crumbled, and Kestrel began nibbling at her food. The meat was tough and charred, and she was too annoyed with herself, and too miserable about all that Aiden had said, to feel hungry. She was not sure she could feel worse than she already did, until her brother spoke up again.

"A true Red Hand," he said flatly, "never loses their weapon."

With a flick of his wrist, he hurled her long hunting knife into the ground beside her hip. When she was sleeping, he must have gone back up the ravine to find it.

As she stared at the quivering hilt, it reminded her that she could not let him help her anymore. By binding her wounds and feeding her, he might have already done too much in the minds of the Elders. Just in case, she flung aside the charred bit of rabbit as if it were a hot ember.

Aiden laughed at her.

CHAPTER NINE

Since a Potential carried little more than the clothes on their back and a single weapon of choice, Kestrel had to make do with the tattered, soaking wet clothes she wore, which did nothing to help against the fever-chills that had come rushing back soon after she got to her feet and began preparing for their long march home.

Aiden suffered no such restrictions, and carried a knapsack full of supplies, a bow, and a quiver of arrows. After he ran a short knife across his scalp, jaw, and chin, she watched jealously as he changed into dry doeskin trousers and a dark green roughspun shirt. Kestrel had a few of those shirts at home, but they did her no good here.

After settling the pack on his shoulders and cinching the straps tight, he gave her a disinterested look. "Ready?"

"I should go on alone," she answered. He might have helped her, but she did not need to let him keep doing so.

A malicious, teasing light came into his eyes.

"A little late for that, isn't it? After all, I already saved you. If I have to again, what difference does it make?"

Kestrel clenched her jaw to keep from screaming, *"I don't want your help!"*

Again, as if reading her mind, he added, "If it makes you feel better, I promise I won't help anymore ... unless you ask."

She had never been able to outmaneuver him, and she was too tired and too sick to try now. "Just go."

He shrugged indifferently, and set out along a game trail running along the grassy bank of the stream. She could never hate Aiden, no matter what he did to her, no matter how little he thought of her, but right now, she very much disliked him.

Kestrel settled the waterlogged hide bundle under her arm, as Aiden moved away through the dripping brush. *I could turn and go some other way,* she told herself, but just the thought of climbing up to the ridgeline she had run along the day before made her legs flutter. She gusted a heavy sigh and, seeing no better choice, went after him.

Within a hundred strides, Kestrel knew this was going to be one of the hardest, longest days of her life. All the wobbliness that had been in her limbs the day before fell on her again, and soon her wounds grew hot to the touch, even through the bandages. She bowed her head, hoped the

Ancestors' blessings remained with her, and walked.

One step led to another, and another after that.

Hours passed.

The day grew bright and warm. The stream gurgling along beside the game trail became wider and wilder, until it tumbled over a drop and fell as a frothy veil to a wide, ferny glade surrounded by towering cedars a hundred feet below. A doe and her fawn drank at the edge of the water. At any other time, Kestrel would have counted it a charming place, but she was having a hard time concentrating on anything, save the desire to sit down and rest.

When Aiden began wading across the stream, she gazed at him with bewilderment. "Home is to the south. Why are you going north?"

"You probably shouldn't come with me," he called over his shoulder. "Just take your Kill, and go to the River. The way you're fumbling around, I'll catch up soon enough."

Kestrel found enough defiance left to meet his challenge—she had no doubt that's what it was—and plunged into the stream after him.

He shook his head and moved on.

Before she climbed onto the opposite bank, she took a long drink, the cold water soothing her dry throat. She wanted to throw herself in and cool her fever, but that would have to wait.

They walked perhaps another mile, climbing up

and over a low ridgeline draped in stands of fir and pine. Squirrels chittered back and forth to one another from high branches, while birds swooped and turned, catching insects in midflight.

When a grouse exploded from a bush in a flurry of beating wings, Aiden snatched an arrow from the quiver at his hip, nocked it to the bowstring, and drew. Just before the bird vanished behind cover farther down the slope, he let fly.

Kestrel watched with a magical sense of awe as grouse and arrow became one. She had often seen the same stunning skill from her brother during the village's Seedtime festivals, after the howling white storms of winter had fled the land, and the ground grew warm enough to plant. Most of the villagers were fair hands with bows, but Aiden had been winning archery contests since he was twelve. He was at his most deadly, however, when holding a pair of long knives, whether they were wooden ones used in mock battles, or the two of steel he had used on the Stone Dogs the night before.

Aiden left her standing on the trail to retrieve the grouse, then returned a few minutes later with the bird hanging from his belt. They set off again.

Over the next hour, Kestrel became aware that her fever had faded a little, and her head was clearing. The gashes the lion had given her still throbbed, but she expected that. Even if the poultices Aiden had placed over the wounds stopped

57

the flesh-rot before it began, the lion's claws had done a nasty job, and the injuries would remain tender for a long time. Kestrel knew, as well as Aiden did, that she owed her life to him. She was grateful, but also suspicious. Even if others never seemed to notice, she was well aware that Aiden never gave something unless he stood to gain more in return. She wondered if this side journey might be leading her to his price.

Around midday, they came to an area where a long ago wildfire had cleared out the forest, providing a view of a wide valley, and beyond that, the scrubby foothills marched off to the east until they joined a dusty, summer-yellow plain.

The valley below them held another of the desolate cities that had not seen human inhabitants since the Red Fever crushed the world.

From their vantage point the leaning, cone-shaped buildings of the city resembled tired old men gathered around their own graves. Sadness touched her heart, but she promptly buried it before Aiden could see her feelings written across her face.

"What are we doing here?" Kestrel asked.

Aiden gave her a strange look. What she saw in his raised eyebrows, too-wide eyes, and slightly parted lips, was a startled uncertainty. She would not have been more surprised if he had fallen over dead at her feet. He spoke quietly, as if imparting a secret. "Have you ever wanted to explore the old cities?"

"No," Kestrel said, aghast. "Everyone knows they are cursed with poisoned luck and dark spirits. More than that, the Elders have forbidden us to enter them. Who in their right mind would want to explore...?"

She trailed off, suddenly understanding his earlier expression. To Aiden, rules were not meant to be broken, and he viewed anyone who so much as bent the rules to be weak and unworthy. And yet, here he was, unable to resist the allure of breaking one such rule.

Maybe the fever was influencing her, but all at once she felt closer to him than she ever had before. For the first time, she saw him as a real person, instead of a piece of walking iron. Seeing him that way, not necessarily fragile, but vulnerable, gave her an idea that never would have crossed her mind before—she had meant every word about the dangers that lurked in the old cities.

"I'll go with you," she said slowly, hoping she was not condemning herself to some gruesome end, "but only if you stop saying I'm not worthy to be a Red Hand."

His brow furrowed in thought. Whatever was going on inside his head seemed disagreeable, but after a few seconds he nodded. "All right, I agree."

His assurance did not sound very convincing, but she decided to take what she could get. "Let's go."

He studied her for a few moments, as if suspecting some trick, then began walking toward the city.

Kestrel went after him, but the closer they came to the outskirts, the less certain she was of the bargain she had made. Thinking again of how he always managed to come out ahead, she could not help but wonder if he had planned this all along.

CHAPTER TEN

Shaped like a huge teardrop, the narrowest point of the ancient city began high up the valley and swelled as it fell into the lower end a few miles away. Gray ribbons, edged with pale lines that magnified the sunlight, formed a gridwork throughout the city. Kestrel knew they were not ribbons at all, but ancient roadways that remained untouched by countless deep snowfalls and spring thaws.

Most such thoroughfares did not extend past the old cities, but when hunting two summers ago, Kestrel had ventured far south of her village. After climbing a high plateau, she had found a similar grid nestled amongst the sage flats. To her, it looked as if someone had thought to build a city on that spot, but had only managed to build the roads.

She had approached the outermost road with superstitious dread. After spending several minutes looking down at the roadway, she talked herself into to touching it, hesitantly at first, like a cat testing water with its paw, then pressing her palm flat against the surface. It had felt like glass, maybe polished stone, but slightly gritty. It had also been cool, despite the heat of the day. When she later told One-Ear Tom about her find, he warned her to stay away. And so she had ... until last winter.

Telling herself that she was only hunting antelope, she returned to the plateau, its smooth crown swept by icy winds and covered in a few inches of snow—except where the roads lay. They were bare, and when she put her hand on one that time, it had been warm and dry. Suspecting some enchantment at work, she had fled.

Now Kestrel and Aiden followed a similar road into the old city. She tried not to think about the coolness of it beneath her feet, despite the beating sun.

They made their way deeper into what had once been home to innumerable people, those who had last walked in the flesh before the Red Fever had, according to One-Ear Tom's more grisly stories, devoured their insides and left them spewing blood in their final moments. What drying bones there might have once been to mark their passing, had long since been dragged away by scavenging animals, or reduced to dust by countless long years.

"I don't like it here," Kestrel said, helpless to avoid speaking aloud her fears. Her eyes traced the evidence of the last wildfire that had swept through the area, probably back before her parents had begun their courtship. Besides old dead tree stumps hidden amongst the new growth, she saw where fingers of flame had shattered windows, and left behind sooty slashes up the sides of almost every nearby building. Rusted corpses of bizarre machines slumped along the roadsides, the wonders they had performed forgotten, and now serving no greater purpose than to provide shelter for rodents. It was hard to believe this city had ever been filled with light and life.

"There's nothing to fear," Aiden said, running his hand over the rusted hulk of a machine that, if the stories were true, might have once soared through the air, or raced at great speed over the land. Kestrel was never sure if those tales were reliable, because some even claimed that people had once traveled between the stars.

"I can feel them watching," Kestrel said softly, recalling a recurring nightmare she used to have. In it, shapeless *things* ripped loose from the muddy ground after a rainstorm—much like the one the night before—and hounded her though a phantom forest cloaked in shadow and mist. No matter how far or fast she ran, those rotting things always caught her. What she remembered clearest about the dream was the way the malignant creatures would ogle her with dead white eyes as they snaked their dead fingers around her throat. Before she woke, their gaping mouths, puffing the reek of things lying putrid in the sun, would fall on her and begin to feed. The memory of their sightless stares and loathsome touch felt much the same as she did now: trapped and afraid.

Aiden favored her with a puzzled look. "Who can you feel?"

"The *dead*. They are everywhere ... watching ... waiting."

Aiden paused. "You mean the *Ancestors?*"

"Who else?"

"They will not trouble us."

"How do you know?"

"Because," Aiden said, "no matter what anyone says, they were just people—like me and you." He spoke as if he had some secret knowledge.

"Maybe they *were* people," Kestrel allowed, "but now they're dead."

"Dead or alive, they will not trouble us."

Kestrel was not so sure. "You know what One-Ear Tom says?"

"Remind me," Aiden answered in a bored tone.

"'The dead want only one thing from the living, and that's to make them dead, too.'"

"If the Ancestors wanted to harm us, then why do we waste our time asking favors of them?"

Kestrel frowned at the raw slash on her palm, from which her blood sacrifice had run. Like it or not, Aiden had a point. If she had trusted the Ancestors enough to give such an offering, in return for ensuring that the lion continued pursuing her, how could she fear them?

"I still don't like being here."

"We won't be for long," Aiden said, leading her to a enormous, circular green. Cracked brickwork paved its edge, and the overgrown grassy center was dotted with stone benches resting under old, hoary trees. A quick glance told her the green was easily twice as large as her village. It seemed that everything about the old world had been huge.

At the center of the green stood a tall metal statue of a stern-faced man looking east. Webs of greenish corrosion covered every inch of him, along with generous splatters of bird droppings on his shoulders and head. A few of the offending birds in question, half a dozen pigeons, cooed and shifted on his shoulders. They were cautious of the two intruders, but not overly frightened. Kestrel wondered if they had seen people here before. If so, who? Brow knotting, she cast a suspicious eye on her brother.

"You've come here before, haven't you?"

He started, as if he had not expected her to guess his secret. His face smoothed, and he stopped under a weeping willow, it hanging bows brushing one of the stone benches. "Several times. Now, until I get back, stay here."

"Where are you going?" Kestrel demanded, failing to hide her unease that he was planning to leave her.

"Don't worry, little sister. You'll be safe ... unless any bears are about to catch the scent of that bloody bundle you're carrying."

Kestrel hugged her prize a little closer. It was beginning to smell ripe. "I'm not afraid of bears."

Aiden flashed a smile that was only about half as scornful as usual. "Then sit down and rest. I'll be back soon."

"You still haven't told me where you're going."

"You'll know soon enough," he said, dropping his knapsack on the ground near the bench. With that, he trotted away.

She watched him until he vanished into a patch of thick bracken and ferns growing between a pair of broken gray buildings on the far side of the green.

CHAPTER ELEVEN

Kestrel drained most of her waterskin before taking a seat on the bench, its stone edges softened by time. It was surprisingly comfortable. So comfortable that she could not resist stretching out and looking up at the sky. The longer she rested there, the farther away her fears soared, and she was able to close her eyes and doze.

She came awake after what felt like just a few minutes, and saw that Aiden had returned. He was stuffing something into his knapsack. She had never seen such a device, but for some reason it sparked a faint memory.

Kestrel sat up and, for a moment, the world spun around her. "What is that?" she asked after the spinning ceased, and armed her sweat-slicked brow. The fever had come back stronger, and she was thirstier than ever. That worried her, because sometimes the worst sicknesses came in waves, each wave stronger than the last. Home was a long way away, and to feel this miserable made that journey seem insurmountable.

Aiden drew what he was holding back out of the pack. "It's a weapon," he said in a reverent hush.

Kestrel croaked a laugh. She knew weapons—bows and spears, axes and knives—but what he held looked like nothing more than a piece of old junk, something that even Fat Will, the village blacksmith, would deem useless.

Aiden scowled. "It *is* a weapon," he insisted, holding it up. It was made of black metal with worn areas along prominent edges that gleamed dull gray. The curved grip seemed built to fit into the palm, just as he was holding it, and the other end, a tapered cylinder with long ridges running along its length, all glowing with a sickly green light, stretched a foot or more from his hand.

As Kestrel studied it, she realized why it was so familiar. "It's a...." she searched for the word she had once heard, "....a *pistol*." There was something more she was missing, something she had found frightening as a little girl when listening to tales around the village green, but she could not remember.

"Yes!" Aiden said, jumping to his feet. She had never seen him let his guard down enough to show so much excitement. "A *firelance* pistol. Watch this," he said, bowing his head over the weapon with a disconcerting familiarity. He flipped a small lever on the side, pointed it at the statue, and slowly squeezed another lever on the underside of the firelance.

Not a lever, Kestrel thought, as a powerful image filled her mind of One-Ear Tom's grizzled face washed in firelight as he declared in somber tones, *The hounds of war squeezed the triggers of their firelances, and brought forth the thunders of Hell from their barrels....*

Eyes widening in alarm, Kestrel looked back to her brother, saw his grimace of anticipation as his finger tightened on the *trigger*. She recoiled in preparation of some roaring—

The weapon made an insignificant clicking noise.

Kestrel let out a shuddering breath. The sweat on her brow now had nothing to do with fever.

Aiden lowered the weapon, a scowl knotting his features. "What's wrong with this thing?"

He fiddled with the lever on the side again, and then Kestrel heard a mosquito-like whine. Smiling now, Aiden lifted the firelance once more. This time when he pulled the trigger, the weapon bucked in his hand, and a whooshing pulse of something—to Kestrel it looked like a fist-sized ball of shimmering air—erupted from the end of the barrel, streaked across the park, and slammed against the head of the statue with a small cracking noise that sent the pigeons winging into the sky, seemingly unhurt.

Impressive, she considered, *but hardly the thunders of Hell*. For a weapon that was supposedly so deadly, it seemed rather harmless.

Aiden appeared to share her opinion. "That's not right," he muttered, fiddling with the side lever again. The mosquito whine was louder this time, and cycling higher. With an almost offhanded gesture, he aimed at the statue and squeezed the trigger.

The second blast, this one tinged like green fire, hit the statue with a thudding roar that ripped through the park, and sent Kestrel diving under the bench, her hands cupped over her ears.

When she dared open her eyes, she saw a cloud of acrid dust drifting away from the statue—rather, what was left of it. Half of it was simply gone. The other half, a twisted, smoky wreckage from the waist down, leaned sharply on its stone pedestal.

Aiden loosed an excited whoop and danced in a circle, looking like a little boy. She had never seen him behave that way, and that unnerved her almost as much as the thought of roaming spirits. He composed himself quickly, but the image remained in her mind, one part endearing, and one part oddly terrifying.

"What do you mean to do with that thing?" Kestrel asked. *Kill Stone Dogs and Black Ears*, he would say. *What else?*

But he did not say that at all.

Aiden squared his shoulders. "I will lead a raid against the Tall Ones."

"*What?*" she demanded, sure the ringing in her ears had made her misunderstand.

"Every old city I've explored has hidden vaults filled with firelances—pistols *and* rifles."

"How many of the old cities have you explored?"

He went on as if she had not spoken. "Some of the vaults hold machines of old, though they look new-made. Hundreds, Kes, maybe thousands of them! But I don't need those machines. With a few of these," he finished, brandishing the firelance, "we can destroy the Tall Ones."

Kestrel's eyes bulged. "Are you mad?" she blurted, getting to her feet. "Why would you attack the Tall Ones?"

"Because they shelter behind their walls, little sister, with no worry of attack. They prowl the darkest nights, and carry away the unwary. Their presence alone fills strong hearts with distress, but I say we should fear this mysterious enemy no more." He spoke with the same veiled dread she always heard when someone mentioned the Tall Ones. But there was something more in his voice, something she had heard from him before, but could not quite recognize.

"Those are all good reasons why they should remain untroubled," she cautioned.

He shook his head, denying her advice. "I want to learn if they are evil spirits, as One-Ear Tom says.

71

I want to learn what devilry they are hiding, discover what powers they wield. These are the things I will find out. And whatever keeps them safe, we will take for ourselves, and use to keep our people safe."

When he said *I will find out*, his voice cracking with conviction, she remembered that he had sounded the same way on the day he told their parents he would become the youngest Red Hand ever, and again when he proclaimed that he would become the youngest warchief. In the end, he had been right, but no one had ever doubted him. The way he sounded now, the way he looked, his eyes hard and cold as ice, told her he wanted more than his words suggested. *But what more is there?*

Aiden stepped close, caught her shoulders, and glared into her eyes as if she were his enemy. "Say nothing about any of this. Do you understand?"

Kestrel hid the wince of pain as his fingers clamped tighter on her shoulders, and nodded.

He held her stare for a long, dreadful minute. "Good. Now, let's get you home. Your fever seems to be getting worse." He flashed a thin, loveless smirk. "I couldn't live with myself if my little sister died in my care."

CHAPTER TWELVE

The Kill, a soggy mess of skin and bone, blood and fur, filled Kestrel's nose with a fearsome reek. It seemed to gain weight with every step she took, until it felt as if she were carrying a bundle of heavy stones. More troubling, her fever was savaging her like a starving predator. One minute she was shaking with cold, the next burning. As the forest began to thin and the steepness of the mountains gave way to rugged hills dotted with scrub brush, an intrusive exhaustion sank deeper into her mind, until she felt snared inside an unsettling dream where neither the world nor its colors were as they should be.

Doggedly, Kestrel put one foot in front of the other, refusing to complain. She snatched handfuls of berries where she found them, crammed them into her mouth, chewed and swallowed. She felt no hunger, and the berries tasted sour, but she had to eat to keep her strength up. As well, she drank deeply from her waterskin, hoping it would not run dry before they reached the river.

Aiden held silent along the march, but he occasionally favored her with his usual disdainful looks. She ignored him. It was easy to do. That way she felt, he might have been a ghost guiding her along.

Dusk had fallen by the time they came to the river, a concrete canal a mile wide and two hundred feet deep. The sloping sides had stairways that led down to deeper pathways, until reaching the water far below.

Her people told that the Ancestors directed the streams flowing off the mountains into this canal, which in turn fed smaller canals. It was said that the world was covered in such canals, moving water from one place to another as needed, eliminating worry over drought. No one knew if canals actually covered the world, but if you followed them long enough, they all eventually led to the impassible boundary of the Dead Lands.

Kestrel knew many such stories of the Ancestors' genius. Stories of how they had tamed the world by eradicating war and famine; how they had survived ages of ice, when the sun stopped giving its light and heat, and the seas froze, and the mountains became trapped under snow. And when the sun burned too bright and too hot, scorching the land, they had persevered and even flourished by building the canals.

Yes, she knew the stories, but the one that

always stayed with her was that of the Ancestors' demise.

Although the they had found ways to stave off sickness and death, and so were able to live lives measured in hundreds of years, the pestilence named the Red Fever devoured them as fire devours straw, leaving their mighty works and machines to churn on and on, until they exhausted the unknowable fuel that drove them, or their metal insides of gears and cogs and springs simply ground themselves into dust.

"So much lost ... so much forgotten," Kestrel murmured, gazing with glassy eyes at the water below, running placid but swift. Every turning of the moon the river flooded, whether it was in the middle of summer or the heart of winter, and the roaring flow would climb almost to the top edge of the canal, scouring it clean.

"What?" Aiden asked, his tone sharp.

"But not *everything* is lost," Kestrel said, feeling at once heavy and light, somehow separate from herself, and yet at the same time buried so deeply within herself that nothing else existed. She smiled wanly. "The ghosts of yesterday still work to keep the river clean. At least we still have that."

Aiden squinted a thoughtful eye at her. "Your fever is getting worse."

Kestrel stared down at the water, wondering if it was cool enough to steal the boiling heat from her blood. "A bath would be nice."

"Kes?"

She took a shaky, swaying step toward a set of stairs.

"Kestrel!" Aiden snapped, lurching towards her.

She dodged out of reach. "You cannot help me! You *shouldn't* have helped me. I'm a Red Hand!"

He lifted his hands. "Then go drown yourself, if that's what you want."

"Just a bath," she muttered, struggling to keep her balance on the concrete steps, wondering at the hands—or had it been machines?—that had built them.

She made it down the first flight, paused to catch her breath on the walkway running off in either direction, then continued.

Halfway down the second set of steps, she passed out of slanting red sunlight and into twilight shadow. It was cooler down in the dark, but the memory of the day's warmth radiated off the smooth gray surfaces. A breeze brought with it the mossy smell of the river.

Kestrel stopped again at the next walkway and looked back the way she had come. The sky, now purple, vaulted above her, but Aiden was nowhere in sight. Had he decided to leave without her? If so, that was fine. She did not need his help, nor did she want it.

Kestrel began down the third flight of stairs, and stiffened between one step and the next, arms held out as she tottered between keeping her balance and falling headlong down the stairs. Before her hung a distorted image of herself. She slowly thrust her head forward, stunned, and saw her mouth yawn impossibly wide in the curved surface. It took a few seconds for her to understand that she was looking into a hovering spherical mirror.

It's not real, she thought. *It can't be.*

But it was, and it was coming closer.

By now, a series of rippling rings were spreading across the smooth surface, making her reflection waver and wobble. From the spot where the ripples originated, a long needle eased out of the sphere.

Kestrel drew back, not daring to breathe. A faint clicking noise came from the sphere, followed by a hum, and then more clicks.

Faster than she could react, the needle shot forward and stabbed the center of her forehead. She reeled drunkenly, her skull ringing as if Fat Will had hit her with one of his hammers. Bursts of light flared and sizzled before her eyes, blotting out everything else.

Aiden called out, seemingly miles away.

"Help me!" Kestrel shrieked, dropping the bundled lion hide and raising her hands for balance. The lights burning across her vision became explosions of crimson, and the ringing agony in her skull deepened, flowed down into her spine like molten metal. Her limbs began to jitter.

"Kes?"

"*HELP ME!*"

"Stay there! I'm coming!"

Kestrel tried to hold still, but it was as if her body had been invaded by a nest of writhing serpents. Her skin burned and itched and crawled. She screamed again, eyes bulging sightlessly.

Aiden called out once more, but his voice was receding.

She was falling. Falling and tumbling down the side of the canal. Down and down and down.

Blackness followed, but did not last.

She found herself looking up at the outline of a bird wheeling through the darkening sky. Then Aiden's face was hovering over hers, blocking out everything else. He was saying something, but she could not hear him. She tried to answer, but her throat had quit working.

And then Aiden began to disappear under seething waves of gray-black flowers, and she felt herself slipping away, suffocating.

She fell into a nightmare filled with fiery pain and swirling images, a place where time had no meaning. Every time she blinked, she saw something different.

Once she saw the night sky, dusted with a

sweep of brilliant stars. The next time she opened her eyes, the soft golden light of dawn had come, but she was looking down at one of the smooth concrete walkways lining the sides of the canal. Aiden's heels flashed, one after the other, in and out of her line of sight. There was a painful pressure in her middle, as she bounced with his every stride. *He's carrying me*, she thought with dazed amazement ... and drifted away.

She opened her eyes and it was full dark again. Aiden was standing in front of her, shoving some bulbous, smelly bundle into her hands.

My Kill, she thought dully. It was so heavy now, and so large that she could barely wrap her arms around it. Kestrel almost let it fall, but a second thought made her hold it tight. *I must keep it safe.*

He spun her around. "Go, Kes," he whispered against her ear. "Go home. You know the way. And remember, say nothing of the old city. For your life, Kes, remember that, and go home." He shoved her forward.

And away she went, staggering, tripping, falling, getting up time and again along a familiar trail. *The way home.*

Her skin burned; her bones felt cracked and charred. The smell of pine sap and evergreen boughs filled her nose, and she wanted nothing more than to lie down and sleep. Instead, she walked into an enveloping black curtain, hearing her brother's whisper: *Go home ... home ... home.*

When last she opened her eyes, Kestrel was again looking straight up. Dark tree branches blocked out most of the stars. She blinked, and then there were a dozen faces staring down at her; hungry faces made freakish and sinister by dancing firelight.

"No more fire," she gasped.

Their hands reached, but they did not *reach* so much as stretch, growing thin and long, like strands of cake batter. Their faces began to ooze and drip.

Kestrel howled. And when those sticky, clutching fingers touched her, she thrashed and clawed, but could not drive them back. They caught hold of her, and she knew there would be no waking after this. No blinking away the nightmare. No retreating into the darkness. She was going to die.

CHAPTER THIRTEEN

"You're awake."

Kestrel started. Until her mother spoke, she had not been consciously aware that she had been awake for some time, watching in a dreamy daze as a spider stalked a fly across the rough slat boards of her bedroom ceiling. She did not feel ill—a little weak, but otherwise well—and it was obvious she had not been devoured by the walking horrors that had found her. *It was all a fever-dream*, she thought, relieved.

She rolled her head on the pillow and looked at her mother. "How long have I been here?"

Tessa stopped a stride from the bed. She held a steaming stoneware cup in one hand. Using the other hand, she pushed her dark hair over her shoulder. The sunlight coming through the window flecked the loose strands with copper. A worry-line formed between her eyebrows. "Four days."

"Four!" Kestrel flung back her blankets and sat up. A bandage under her nightgown shifted on her hip, but other than a slight tightness in the muscles, there was little pain. The same held for her shoulder, belly, and calf.

"The flesh-rot wasn't too bad, was it?" she asked in a worried voice. "You didn't have to ... *cut* anything away, did you?"

A hesitant smile crossed Tessa's lips. "There was no flesh-rot. Your wounds needed cleaning and fresh poultices, but no more than any others I've tended. If anything, I've never seen such wounds heal so quickly and cleanly. Of course, you'll have scars. There's no helping that."

No flesh-rot? "But what about the fever? I didn't imagine that." Kestrel shuddered as hazy memories paraded across her mind. She saw Aiden slaughtering the Stone Dogs, the old city where he had found the firelance pistol, and the river at dusk.

"Your fever had nothing to do with flesh-rot," Tessa said, taking another hesitant step closer. The worry-line on her brow deepened. "Perhaps you drank some bad water, or ate a poison berry."

For the first time, Kestrel truly noticed how her mother was behaving, not just concerned, but hesitant. Kestrel could guess why. Aiden must have gone back on his word, and told everyone he helped her.

It took a moment for Kestrel to find the words to express her regret, which sounded inadequate in her mind, and somehow offhanded, despite their sincerity. It took a longer moment to get them out in the open.

"I'm sorry for bringing shame upon our family."

Tessa blinked. "What are you talking about?"

Kestrel appreciated her mother's kindness, but sometimes the woman refused to accept the truth before her eyes.

"If I've been here four days," Kestrel began, "then everyone knows Aiden brought me home, and that I—" she closed her eyes against a sudden, burning sting "—that I failed."

"You didn't fail. Far from it." Her mother edged closer, lifted a comforting hand, but stopped short of laying it on Kestrel's brow. The hint of trepidation Kestrel had noticed had become more evident.

"Aiden should've left me to die," Kestrel said, "but he didn't. I'm surprised I've not been banished already."

Despite her obvious reluctance to do so, Tessa came closer and placed her wrist against Kestrel's forehead. She pulled back, frowning. "You're cool ... but then, sometimes the worst fevers leave people confused long after they have run their course."

Kestrel ground her teeth together. "It's not the fever. I failed!"

After that, everything spilled out in a bitter flood. "I killed the lion, but then Stone Dogs chased me. If it hadn't been for Aiden, they would've cut me to pieces. Then we...."

She trailed off to silence. Aiden had warned her

not to say anything about the old city, the firelances, or his intention to attack the Tall Ones. As murky as her memories were, she remembered all too well how he had looked into her eyes, as if she were an enemy. More than anything in the world, she wanted to avoid crossing her brother, out of both love and fear. As to the hovering, mirror-like sphere that had poked her, a quick brush of her fingertips informed her there was not so much as a bump on her forehead, so there was no question in her mind that it had been part of her fever-dream, much like the vision of the villagers melting before her eyes.

"Kes ... what is it?"

"We escaped to the river. By then, my fever was worse, and Aiden must have carried me home."

Tessa shook her head with bemusement. "If that's what you *think* happened, you were sicker than we all thought. Lie down and rest."

"Stop trying to make me feel better!"

Tessa's face hardened. "Sick or not, you will not raise your voice to me. Now, lie down!"

Chastened, Kestrel obeyed. Aiden had suggested their mother was weak, and that being a farmer was a disgrace to their family, but Tessa was no night flower that would wilt under the sun's first rays. When she gave a command, there was no defying it. Kestrel was sure that if her mother had chosen to become a warrior, she would have succeeded. But Tessa had always quietly disapproved of the needed brutality of a Red Hand's life. It was one thing for the son or daughter of some other villager to become a Red Hand, but quite another for her own children—especially Kestrel—to choose that path.

Tessa pulled the blankets back under Kestrel's chin. "You did not fail," she said firmly. "Nor did you bring shame to our family,"

"A Potential can have no help," Kestrel said woodenly.

"You didn't have any help to do ... what you did."

Kestrel laughed bitterly, knowing now that Tessa was only trying to protect her, as she always had. "If Aiden didn't help me, then I must've lost my mind somewhere up in the mountains." She glanced sharply at her mother. "Maybe I'm still there, and you are not real?"

"I'm as real as you are." Tessa pulled a stool closer to the bed and sat down. She smoothed her earth-colored roughspun dress with the hands of a much older woman. A lifetime of working the fields had left her fingers cracked and calloused. They looked hard, tough as old leather—far more so than Kestrel's. When Tessa spoke again, she did so in a lowered voice.

"None of the Elders believed you needed an observer, but after scouts reported finding signs of a raiding party, I convinced them, with One-Ear

Tom's help, to send Aiden. He told us that by the time he reached your chosen battleground, you had already come and gone. He found the evidence of the Kill, and trailed you to the village. He almost caught up with you, but the guards found you first, after you staggered up to the River Gate."

Kestrel lay there, hearing Aiden speak in her mind. *Once you hang the bones of your Kill around your neck,* Aiden spoke from within her mind, *you'll be counted as a Red Hand. And if there's one thing all Red Hands are expected to do, it is to fight our enemies. When your first battle comes, and you begin weeping and shaking like you did over that lion, everyone will know that you are not a true Red Hand, and never were...."*

So he had kept his word after all, but that did not keep a wave of anger from washing over Kestrel. *I will prove him wrong!*

Only if you go along with his lies, a different voice countered. *And if you do so, you will become a liar, the same as him.*

Guilt replaced anger, but she promptly crushed it down. She had made a blood sacrifice to the Ancestors, and they had responded by putting the lion into her hands for the Kill. If they had done that much, why would they have taken it all back by letting the Stone Dogs capture her?

They wouldn't have, she thought, growing more sure of that the longer she mulled it over. *The*

Ancestors would've given me a way to escape my enemies, or they would've helped me overcome them.

In that light, Aiden's meddling did not matter. Considering it all together, Kestrel found only one conclusion: *I am a Red Hand, and soon everyone will know it—even Aiden!*

Filled with a new sense of determination, Kestrel once more flung her blankets aside.

"What are you doing?" her mother demanded.

Kestrel dropped her feet to the floor. "I must prepare for the Bone Tree ceremony."

Tessa pushed her back. "You're not strong enough to endure the trials of the ceremony." What she did not say was plainly reflected in her gaze. *Moreover, you cannot even remember what happened to you.*

"I feel fine," Kestrel said. And while her wounds were still tender, she felt strong and alert. Besides all the rest, the worst part of the Bone Tree ceremony had nothing to do with strength of body, only of the mind. Just thinking about that part sent a shudder through her, and heated her cheeks.

Tessa, still holding Kestrel's shoulders, abruptly flinched back and clutched her hands together in her lap, that uneasy expression of meeting a dangerous stranger back on her face.

Kestrel frowned. "What's the matter with you?"

Before Tessa could say anything, Kestrel's

father burst into the room, followed by Aiden.

"Kes!" Elder Matthias boomed, his voice far larger than his slender frame suggested possible. Displaying none of his wife's caution, he wrapped Kestrel in a smothering hug. His dark beard—short, bristly, and streaked with white—tickled her cheek, and his long hair momentarily obscured her sight.

"Careful," Tessa chided. "You'll tear her wounds."

"Nonsense, woman!" Matthias said. "Our daughter has proven she's far stronger than any of us ever imagined." He cast a sidelong glance at Aiden. "Isn't that right, son?"

Aiden lowered his head. "She made a liar out of me," he said in an abashed tone so sincere that Kestrel almost believed it. When he looked up, however, the familiar teasing light danced in his eyes. It seemed that only Kestrel noticed. "Had I known my little sister was so fearsome, I would've demanded that the Elders allow her to perform the rite of the Kill two years ago."

Matthias arched a quizzical eyebrow. "And risk losing the honor of being the youngest Red Hand?"

Aiden offered a shrug and a modest half-smile.

"You've grown much, my son, from the boy you were. I'm proud of you."

Tessa turned to her husband. "We must let her rest."

"I'm ready for the ceremony," Kestrel said.

Matthias stroked his chin. "If you feel as well as you say, then tomorrow is soon enough—after all, there are preparations to be made."

Tessa shook her head. "Even that is too soon!"

Kestrel's father glanced at his daughter. "You have proven yourself already, so there is no need to hurry things."

Kestrel looked to Aiden's smirking face, and her anger flared. "I will stand beneath the Bone Tree *tonight*," she announced.

"So be it," Matthias said, chest puffed with pride. "Now, daughter, while the day is young, get some sleep. You will need it."

CHAPTER FOURTEEN

Kestrel tried to sleep, but every time she closed her eyes, she thought about the Bone Tree ceremony and all the people gathering to watch her, and they would pop back open.

Eventually she climbed out of bed, dressed herself in the unadorned doeskin dress her mother had made especially for the occasion, and a pair of soft leather slippers. Last, she brushed and braided her dark hair.

It felt good to move around, but the pull of her stitches when she turned or twisted worried her. Kestrel decided there was no changing her mind. By now, her family and the rest of the villagers were already preparing for the festivities that would follow the ceremony. Soon, they would begin looking for her arrival.

Knowing what was required made her skin crawl. *Tonight* everyone *you know will be there watching—*

Kestrel closed her eyes, took a deep breath, and banished all thoughts about what was coming.

For now, it worked.

When she opened her eyes and glanced around the bedroom, she felt as if she was forgetting something. Her father would bring the weapons she needed, along with the bones of her Kill, so other than her clothes and herself, there was nothing else to take.

"You're stalling," she told herself, and almost laughed.

When she had left the village as a Potential, she had done so with much more enthusiasm, and certainly no hesitation. She told herself she had nothing to fear now, but she could not quite believe it. What she would have to do at the Bone Tree ceremony had always terrified her more than anything else about becoming a Red Hand. Until recently, though, those requirements had always seemed distant, trials that were far beyond tomorrow or the next day.

Now she was speeding toward the final moments, and she felt more scared than ever. Her heart had not beaten so hard, nor had her hands shook so much, when she faced the lion or run from the Stone Dogs.

Before panic drove her to dive under the bed, she took a steadying breath and walked purposefully out of her room, passed through her family's dim but cozy cabin, the air fragrant of the venison stew bubbling in an iron pot atop the large cook stove, and stepped outside.

A squirrel shucking seeds from a pinecone eyed her from a sunlit branch, and in a coop set away from the cabin, chickens clucked and scratched to the disinterest of a pair of nanny goats sharing an adjoining pen. Out behind the cabin, farther up the hillside, four pigs rooted and grunted nosily in their slop troughs.

That wasn't so hard, was it? Kestrel thought, letting the sights and sounds of familiar surroundings calm her. Taking another deep breath, she imagined she was only going for a stroll through the forest. Before the serene illusion had a chance to break apart, she set off.

The wooded path she followed began in the shadow of the protective cliffs soaring above the village, ran by her family's home, and then snaked its way down the mountainside, passing several timber-and-stone cabins tucked deep within stands of fir and pine. If she had not known they were there, and if the owners' dogs had not barked at her passing, Kestrel would never have noticed them. Within each cabin resided a Red Hand and their family, or a hunter and theirs. For several generations the loose, well-hidden perimeter had thwarted many surprise attacks that befell the village.

Of course, when raiding parties came howling out of the forest, one need not be a Red Hand or hunter to fight. From a young age, everyone in the village learned how to use any weapon at hand. The difference between a common villager and a Red Hand was that a Red Hand spent their lives learning the tactics of warfare, going on raids, and launchings counterattacks in defense of the village. Becoming a Red Hand was a choice few made, and fewer achieved.

Kestrel lifted a hand in greeting to the people she saw ghosting through the woods. All waved back. Some were other Potentials, young men and women like her who would one day make this very same walk. They were her friends and family, but after tonight, their paths would separate, until they either became Red Hands themselves, or failed and were sent into the Dead Lands. Of all the people she saw, only her mentor, One-Ear Tom, spoke to her.

"Are you ready, young Kes?" The grizzled warrior was leaning against a tree with his arms folded across his chest, as if his only task in life was to watch the world grow older, one day at a time. His long white hair hung over his shoulders, contrasting against his black roughspun shirt. He had seen many and many years, but still had a warrior's powerful bearing.

"Only because of your training," Kestrel said evenly. Skittish as she felt, she was just happy she had not choked on the answer. "Are you ready?"

One-Ear Tom grinned, showing the scant

handful of lonely teeth left to him. "My part in all this is far easier than yours. Though, after what you did," he said with that same glint of approval in his eyes that she had seen in her father's gaze, "I suppose the ceremony will be easy for you."

Kestrel's smile felt brittle. In that moment, she almost told One-Ear Tom the truth about everything. For many years, she had spent more time with him than anyone else, and she trusted him as she would a relative. Aiden's voice spoke up from the depth of memory, and her smile hardened into a rigid slash. *Say nothing about any of this.*

Kestrel waved stiffly and moved down the trail.

On the outskirts of the village, the smell of hot metal and the ring of hammers filled the air. She paused beside an area filled with bristling mountains of rusted iron, twisted steel scrap, and weeds. No matter if you were a farmer, a hunter, or a Red Hand, the villagers collected anything that had potential use and brought it to the blacksmith, Fat Will, and his son, Short Will. Between the two of them, they could transform almost any sort of junk into useful tools or weapons, of one sort or another.

Behind the heaps of rusty scrap rose the cedar-shingled roof of Fat Will's forge, and from its wobbly brick chimney climbed an ever-present plume of smoke. If habit held true, Fat Will would be late to the ceremony. Of all the people in the village, no one worked harder, except for farmers, but even they had the winter months to rest before the next year's planting.

You're stalling again, Kestrel told herself, and left Fat Will to his labor.

The sudden and violent need to vomit coiled through Kestrel's belly as soon as she saw the village wall, a sheer bulwark of stone and earth rising twenty feet in height. In her mind's eye, she imagined the villagers standing watch for her, their faces calm, but their eyes alive with doubt. Far away, in one of the lower summer pastures, a calf bawled for its mother. The sound was at once urgent and forlorn. Kestrel felt a kinship with the poor beast.

"You are a Red Hand," she told herself in harsh tones, and the greasy twisting of her insides slowly eased. She strode through the Mountain Gate and entered the village.

As soon as Kestrel saw how deserted the village was, she felt like a fool. If she had been thinking clearly, she would have known this was what she would find. The real show, after all, was at the Bone Tree.

That's where they'll be waiting. That's where they'll be watching. That's where I'll have to—

The need to spew her last meal struck again, but this time the sensation made Kestrel angry. *Stop this!* she chided herself. *You are Red Hand, and the first enemy a Red Hand slays is fear. Go to the*

95

Bone Tree. Go now, and let all know that you do not fear!

Kestrel obeyed her silent command, and quickly strode along the wide dirt tracks winding through the village. Dogs nosing about for scraps of anything to eat looked up at her passing, wagged their tails, barked happy greetings, then went back to their eternal searches. Ever watchful cats were more elusive, keeping to the shadows between stone and timber buildings, or lurking under two-wheeled carts loaded with everything from firewood to metal scrap bound for Fat Will's forge to wooden buckets loaded with the first berries of summer. She knew the hour was growing late, as red and gold now smudged the evening sky.

Every time her stride slowed, she told herself: *Go!*

Before long she was running, her legs carrying her through a row of timber granaries standing on wooden posts along one side of the village green, across this large open space reserved for festivals and marriage ceremonies, and then through a row of cabins.

Soon after, she passed from the village through the Bald Hill Gate, and sprinted up a forest trail thick with the sweet smell of evergreens, her feet drumming lightly over a carpet of pine straw.

It struck her that she was racing to outpace her fears, while at the same time running straight toward the very thing she feared most. Even as she considered this, she burst into the open field below the Bone Tree and skidded to a halt, panting, nervous eyes darting.

People milled about everywhere. She had known them all her life, but they all looked like strangers.

CHAPTER FIFTEEN

A few villagers might have noticed her abrupt arrival, but most were busy eating, laughing, or trying in vain to wrangle unruly children who were chasing each other about. Again, if she had been thinking straight, she would have remembered this was how it always was ... at least until the actual ceremony began.

Kestrel's gaze climbed briefly above the villagers to the Bone Tree, standing alone atop a large grassy knoll. Knowing what would happen when she stood beneath it, she dropped her gaze, and found her mother talking to Mary, a short plump woman who worked the fields with her. Aiden stood on the opposite side of the clearing, speaking with his band of Red Hands. The other four bands were clustered nearby.

"I was beginning to think you'd changed your mind," said her father, coming closer with a warrior's easy, yet somewhat dangerous gait. His clothing, a black leather vest over a gray roughspun shirt, leather trousers, and soft-soled boots, was similar to what most men wore in the village. His long hair, iron gray at the temples, swept back from his brow, and was held in place at the back with a leather thong. Nothing in his appearance marked him as an Elder—pretension of any sort was frowned upon in the village. Nevertheless, a quiet air of authority surrounded him, and a touch of stateliness.

Kestrel sought an answer, but could not find the words. With no better choice, she showed Matthias her teeth in what she hoped resembled a confident grin, and not a terrified grimace.

"I'd tell you not to be nervous," Matthias said, proving that her expression was less than she had hoped for, "but that's impossible, isn't it?"

"Were you nervous?" Kestrel blurted.

Matthias laughed. "Nervous then, and nervous now. I feel as if I'm about to go through the ceremony myself, instead of you. But you will do fine." His features grew sober. "Have you asked the Ancestors to bless you?"

"Every day for as long as I can remember."

"Do you think they have?"

Kestrel remembered cutting her palm on the mountain, and giving her blood in return for their aid. "Yes. But no one can know the ultimate will of the Ancestors," she said by rote, "until they have returned us safe to hearth and home."

He glanced skyward, and she followed his gaze.

The first stars of the evening twinkled in the far east. To the west, the sky glowed with the last dying fires of sunlight.

"I don't pretend to know the will of the Ancestors," Matthias said, dropping a comforting hand on her shoulder and turning her toward the Bone Tree, "but in you, I have been blessed."

Again, Kestrel could find no words. She wondered what her father would think if he knew Aiden had helped her after the Kill? Disappointment, to be sure, and if not for that, she would have told him right then. Part of her *wanted* to tell him as much as she had wanted to tell One-Ear Tom, but she simply could not tell the truth. She had worked her entire life to become a Red Hand, and it was not fair that Aiden had intervened for the sole purpose of destroying her dream.

Damn him, she thought, and decided that even if her silence displeased the Ancestors, she would take the secret to her grave. She had fought the lion and defeated it. And after, she had nearly gotten away from the Stone Dogs. Aiden's showing up had denied her the chance to defend herself or escape, and she refused to take the blame for that. If either of them were guilty of defying tradition, it was Aiden—he who never went against custom.... *Unless he has something to gain*, she silently amended.

Her father, looking at the Bone Tree, did not seem to notice Kestrel's scowl of concentration.

"The time has come. Go now, daughter, to your purpose."

Kestrel squared her shoulders and stepped away from him. As soon as his hand vanished, a tremendous weight fell upon her, as if he had actually been holding her up.

The villagers saw her marching up the knoll and fell silent. Even the rowdy children went still, much as she had done on many occasions when growing up.

Her heart pounded harder the closer she came to the Bone Tree. One-Ear Tom claimed the great oak, with its thick, serpentine limbs hung with tufts of moss and clacking bones, had stood old and tall when their people first arrived here.

Kestrel could believe it, for the tree's girth was more than a dozen men clasped hand-in-hand could reach around, and its hoary bark was gray and gnarled by countless years. No other tree like it existed in these parts, which gave credence to the idea that it might be a wonder given life by the Ancestors themselves.

At the top of the knoll, the grass gave way to a wide, circular path of quartz gravel, meticulously cleaned of fallen leaves and twigs, and then smoothed with rakes. At the center of the path, just beyond the outer reach of the tree's great limbs, stood a bench carved from black stone and swirled throughout with veins of rich cream. As far as anyone knew, it had been there as long as the Bone Tree, a forgotten monument given new life by her people.

Feeling as if something were pushing and pulling her at the same time, Kestrel crunched over the gravel and halted before the bench.

No one moved at the edges of her sight, but she felt the weight of their stares—a far heavier burden than she had previously imagined. Sweat beaded on her brow, coursed down her spine. Her pulse jumped in her throat.

Her eyes took in the sprawling lower branches above her, then rose higher. Everywhere she looked, bones hung from slender wires. The lowest still looked somewhat fresh. Those a bit higher had been bleached white by the sun. The highest bones were the oldest, and were gray, cracked, and spotted with lichen.

Hundreds of bones, perhaps thousands. The legacy of all the Red Hands who had come before her.

One-Ear Tom told that a group of wretched survivors during the Great Sorrow had gathered on this knoll, below this ancient tree, and had forged an alliance in order that a few might stand together as one against the hardships of the world.

And so had been born the House of the Red Hand. As a warning to all those who thought to attack them, they hung the bones of their vanquished enemies upon the tree. Over time, rival tribes had learned to fear the Red Hands, and their attacks diminished. In turn, the rite of the Kill gradually replaced human bones with the bones of fearsome beasts.

All that changed when, two years before, Aiden had added the skull of a Black Ear. It swung on its wire, the gaping, sightless eyes seeming to stare down at Kestrel. Some counted Aiden's deed as an honor to the original Red Hands. Others, like Kestrel's mother, feared it was an omen of coming trouble. All Kestrel could think was that the bones of her Kill would soon be added to these—

But not soon enough! Kestrel thought in alarm. Her insides cramped, and she feared she was about to make a fool of herself. She swallowed the flood of spit in her mouth, forced herself to breathe slowly and deeply, until the queasiness passed. It was not so easy to hide the heat filling her cheeks. Even from afar, she guessed her face must be glowing red.

It is time, a small voice whispered in the back of her mind.

Kestrel turned to face the villagers, and froze.

The faces were blurred smears all around her. She blinked several times, but they never grew any clearer.

If they are blurry to me, then I must be blurry to them.

It was a thin, unrealistic wish.

She had stood where they did often enough to know anyone in her place stood out with an otherworldly clarity, as if the Ancestors themselves intervened in this act to ensure that only the bravest in all things became a Red Hand.

It is time, the voice said again.

I cannot!

You must.

I ... I ... I must.

Kestrel stared straight ahead, her face rigid as stone. Hands shaking, she bent, caught the bottom of her dress, and carefully pulled it up and over her head. As the dress fell from her fingers, the cooling evening air pebbled her bare skin.

No one laughed or snickered, which had been her greatest fear, but neither did they look away. She stood before them, as naked and defenseless as a newborn, save for the bandages at her neck and hip and belly. According to this part of the ceremony, if there was any fault hidden within her, the Ancestors would make it known to all.

Half sure the Ancestors would strike her dead for keeping Aiden's secrets, Kestrel waited, staring straight ahead, arms spread wide. No boils erupted over her skin, nor did lightning fall from the cloudless twilight sky, nor any of the other gruesome things One-Ear Tom often spoke of during the Reaptime celebration.

In the gathering darkness, the villagers looked

on, giving her their silent support. A day might come when they were as exposed as she was now, and on that day, in her capacity as a Red Hand, they would expect her to repay their support with her skill and courage as a warrior.

Only when the low thrumming of drums sounded, and torches were lit, one by one around the crescent-shaped perimeter formed by the villagers, did Kestrel lower her arms. Letting out a breath that rattled in her throat, she walked around the bench and knelt, facing her people.

The Bone Tree ceremony had begun.

CHAPTER SIXTEEN

One-Ear Tom walked up to Kestrel after she knelt, his tread falling in time with the beat of the drums. He offered Kes a gap-toothed smile. "You did well."

She smiled nervously in return, but said nothing.

He had changed into a long robe the color of fresh blood, and was carrying a wooden tray loaded with stoneware cups. Red smears covered the wide mouths of some. A few of the others held arrays of wooden tool handles of all different lengths.

Kestrel fixated on those handles, all spotted with red fingerprints. "Will it hurt?"

The old warrior set his tray down on the end of the bench, and then picked up the smallest, cleanest looking cup. "After a few sips of seeker's tea, you'll not feel any pain." He held it out to her, his movements precise, solemn. "Drink, young Kes, and learn the will of the Ancestors."

When Kestrel took the cup, she realized that her embarrassment had faded. That was not to say she was comfortable being undressed in front of so many, let alone One-Ear Tom, but her bare skin seemed less important than it had before. The ceremony had nothing to do with desires of the flesh. In place of the discomfort, she had gained a growing sense of confidence and purpose amongst her tribe.

"What will I see?" She had asked the same of her brother and father once, but they had refused to tell. The secret of the seeker's tea was reserved for Red Hands alone.

Instead of answering, One-Ear Tom motioned for her to drink, and she did. The thick liquid was warm and bitter, and she almost gagged. Instead, she managed to drink it all down without so much as a grimace.

After draining the cup, she handed it back with the same reverence in which he had presented it to her.

He took it in his gnarled hands, looked inside, nodded approvingly. "Your brother spewed the first sip back into the cup." One-Ear Tom grinned. "Of course, that meant he had to drink that, too."

While Kestrel found that slightly amusing, she was interested in other matters. "What will I see?" she insisted, alarmed by the sudden, heavy gurgling in her belly.

One-Ear Tom placed the cup back with the others. "Can you keep a secret?" he asked in a conspiratorial hush.

You have no idea, Kestrel thought, even as she nodded.

"I saw *nothing* when I drank the tea," he admitted. "Oh, I felt strange, but I gained no secret knowledge from the Ancestors. I tell you, as I was told on the day I became a Red Hand, and as I've told all who have received the cup from my hand, there is no shame in not hearing from the Ancestors. They are fickle, our guardians, and one should always remember that they dole out blessings and curses according to their will, not ours. I've often suspected that those who claim to have seen some sign, actually saw only what their secret hearts showed them." He shrugged. "But I could be wrong. Either way, if you see something, Kes, you must speak of it at the appointed time."

That was not exactly what Kestrel wanted to hear, but she bowed her head in acceptance.

One-Ear Tom caught her eye. "Can you promise me something?"

"Of course."

"When you wake in the morning, do not hold how you feel against me."

"I won't," she promised, not sure what he was getting at.

"Then let us begin."

Kestrel nodded again, and he took his tray and its burden of cups and tools around behind her, and knelt in the gravel, which had taken on a wintry radiance, like fresh snow reflecting the light of a full moon. But the moon had not yet risen, so there was only faint starlight, and what little was thrown by the distant torches. *Is this the strangeness he mentioned?* If so, it was not so bad.

"Are you ready?" One-Ear Tom asked, his voice deeper than usual, each word dragging.

"Yes," she answered, her own voice booming in her ears.

She glanced up sharply, taking in the faces of the villagers. None seemed startled by her outburst, which made her wonder if she had called out loudly at all.

Her mind shifted.

Where they had looked blurry before, now she could make out their features with freakish clarity, even those standing beyond the flickering torchlight. Not only that, it seemed as if she could hear their breathing, a collective, whispering rush of sound, like a fitful wind pushing through a grove of aspens. She could also hear their heartbeats pounding in tandem with the rhythmic thudding of the drums. It was impossible, but she thought if she listened hard enough, she would actually hear their thoughts.

The seeker's tea is doing this, Kestrel considered uneasily, wanting it to stop, but knowing there was no escape until it had run its course. She fought against the desire to leap to her feet and run away.

I am a Red Hand, and fear is the first enemy I must slay.

She flinched at the feel of small, cold teeth biting into the skin of her shoulder, and they went away.

"Are you *sure* you are ready?" One-Ear Tom asked.

Kestrel's gaze swept around.

The gravel was not just glowing anymore. Tongues of pale flame were leaping off the path's surface, and within those snowy flames she saw long, distorted faces.

Beyond the band of gravel, the swaying grass, such a vibrant green that it hurt her eyes, whispered secrets in a delicate language she could not understand. Over it all, yet perfectly distinct, she heard the rushing gale heaving in and out of the villagers' chests, the thunder of their hearts. The torches dotting the crowd flared with the intensity of small suns, and their heat reached across the field, climbed the flanks of the knoll, and fell on her bare skin, making it tingle.

"Begin," she said, her tone calm, assured.

The teeth returned to nibble her skin, but the pain was less than before. With it came the muffled sound of wood striking wood—*tap-tap-tap-tap*—a sound picked up and intensified by the rattling bones swinging from the ancient oak's boughs.

Kestrel kept her back straight as One-Ear Tom worked, her slitted eyes taking in her surroundings. A flood of images surged over her. She saw herself fighting the lion again, then running from the Stone Dogs. She saw the old city, then the firelance in Aiden's hand devastating the metal statue.

Say nothing about any of this. His voice was thick with menace.

You do not frighten me. I am a Red Hand.

The defiant thought flew from her mind in this vision, just as the shimmering pulse of air had flown from the firelance pistol. Instead of striking a metal man, it struck Aiden in the chest. He exploded into a cloud of glittering dust. Harmless now. Harmless forever.

The tapping ended, the nibbling ceased, and One-Ear Tom said something behind her. His words were garbled. The beating of the drums roared and raged, the wind howled and screamed, bones clacked and rattled, but Kestrel felt only peace within the surreal storm.

Movement caught her eye, and she watched one band of Red Hands separate from the others. Each band had between twenty-five and thirty warriors, few of them women, and they had all donned red robes matching One-Ear Tom's.

The band marched in a line toward the top of the knoll. Her brother was not among them.

Because they were siblings, a rarity amongst the Red Hands, he would come last.

One by one, the Red Hands moved behind her, and the tapping and nibbling against her skin resumed for some immeasurable time, ceased, then began again.

Again and again, until all the bands had come and gone, and only Aiden remained.

He sneered down at her, and she sneered in return.

Scowling, he moved behind her. Where there had been tapping and nibbling before, she heard great hammering booms, felt claws of fire digging into her flesh. He wanted to hurt her, cow her, shame her.

Back straight and rigid as an iron rod, she bore the pain.

And then it was over. One-Ear Tom, with a disparaging look at Aiden's retreating back, helped Kestrel to her feet and brought her around the stone bench.

Kestrel looked down at her people, and they looked up at her, rapt, silent, waiting. When the old warrior turned her around, the silence held a little longer, then the villagers let out a cheer that shook the air.

Though she could not see it herself, Kestrel knew what provoked their jubilant approval. The mark of the Red Hand had been set deep into her skin, and there it would forever remain.

When the cheering died down, One-Ear Tom helped her dress in a snug roughspun shirt that stuck to her bloody back, then leather trousers that stuck to her sweating legs, and finally soft boots. The clothes were more suitable for what was coming, but Kestrel would have been happy if she'd had only bags to wear.

As she straightened from tugging on her last boot, the villagers cheered again, but the lone face she easily picked out belonged to her brother. As always, he was looking at her as if the mere sight of her disgusted him beyond words.

The pride she felt withered in the heat of her anger for Aiden's abuses on this night, and all her life.

The time is fast coming, my brother, when we will face each other below the Bone Tree ... and I promise to show you as much care as you have shown me.

A heady thought, but even with the power of the seeker's tea doing its strange work upon her, she was not sure she had the strength or the will to challenge Aiden. All she could do was try ... and hope she was not about to make the greatest mistake of her life.

CHAPTER SEVENTEEN

Below where Kestrel and One-Ear Tom stood, the Red Hands, marching to the drums' lumbering beat, formed a large ring. The villagers linked hands and made a larger ring around them. Every third person held aloft a torch.

Now the Red Hands peeled off their robes and drew mock weapons—long knives carved from ash trees. After pairing off, their precise movements matching the rhythm of the drums, the ring they had formed began to rotate within the ring formed by the villagers, and as it did, the paired warriors moved through a series of fighting stances. Each strike was countered with a block, their ash weapons slamming together with sharp claps. At first, the sound of those practice weapons coming together was chaotic, but quickly took on its own hypnotic cadence.

"Careful, young Kes," One-Ear Tom said, studying her face.

She shifted her gaze from Aiden to him. The seeker's tea was still at work in her, but the otherworldly sensations had dissipated. What she felt now was an uncanny clarity of mind. "What do you mean?"

"I assume you've chosen who you will challenge?"

"I have," Kestrel said. Thinking on it now, she had always known whom she would fight, just as she had always known whose band she wanted to join. "Aiden."

One-Ear Tom pursed his lips, and his brow gained a few thoughtful wrinkles. "If you do this, you know it will not be just for show."

"I do," Kestrel said without hesitation. "I don't want it any other way."

"Your brother is not a man to make into an enemy."

"He has given me no choice." She cocked a thumb and gestured toward her back. The force he had used to hammer the ink into her skin was needless, and she could feel trickles of blood oozing down her shoulder blade.

"I'd be honored to fight you, as would your father, and both choices follow custom."

"I will fight Aiden, and prove myself to him and his band."

He caught her shoulders. "Do not believe that his harsh ways with you are anything but love."

"Love?" Kestrel spat, wrenching herself free of her teacher's grip.

"Yes, *love*. Being a Red Hand is not the same as growing crops, or working with leather, wood, and metal. It is a dangerous life, merciless and brutal. To be a warrior is to make few true friends, because most everyone you know eventually ends up dead or maimed. Perhaps, in his own way, Aiden wanted to spare you from that burden."

Kestrel did not know what to say. No one she knew had ever spoken so unfavorably of being a Red Hand, and surely not One-Ear Tom. Of course, she knew people died in battle, but always their deaths were celebrated and revered by villagers and Red Hands alike. Only the survivors of battle received more honor—and that, she was sure, was really at the heart of her brother's cruelty toward her, not love.

"Aiden's desire is not to spare me," she said, her features stiff, "but to keep me from ever having the chance to dim the light of his glory."

"Perhaps," One-Ear Tom said with a resigned sigh. He reached behind his back, drew a pair of long wooden knives from his belt, and placed them in her waiting hands. "If you *are* right, then your task is all the more dangerous, because when you call him out, he'll know why you have broken tradition."

He glanced toward the ring of fighting Red Hands, then back to her. "Aiden fights boldly, fearlessly, as you must know."

Kestrel nodded, for she did know, and all the more after seeing him slaughter the Stone Dogs who had chased her.

"Any weakness on your part—"

"I am not weak!"

One-Ear Tom fixed her with a piercing stare. "No, but right now you are behaving like a spoiled child."

"Forgive me," Kestrel said, and meant it. Only disappointing her father was more troubling to her than disappointing One-Ear Tom.

"I've never been a good teacher, girl, but heed what I tell you, or you'll end up spending your first months as a Red Hand recovering in a sickbed."

Kestrel knew he was only being modest. One-Ear Tom was one of the finest teachers in the village, and everything she knew of fighting had come at his instruction. She nodded reluctantly, once more the pupil, if only for a short time.

"He will attack straight away, hoping to intimidate you. Become the rabbit, and let him *see* your fear—"

"You sound like my mother," Kestrel said, unable to believe this was his guidance.

One-Ear Tom smiled wryly. "Has Tessa ever given you bad advice?"

Kestrel opened her mouth, then snapped her teeth together. "No," she said after a moment, "but what does showing fear have to do with fighting

Aiden?"

He shrugged. "Maybe everything, maybe nothing. But if our places were reversed, that's how I would fight him. Using his confidence against him is the only advantage you have. And you had best make good use of it, because this fight will be as close to the real thing as you dare get without sharp steel in your hands."

Kestrel thought it would have been better if her teacher had said nothing and let her go blindly forward. "I have to fight him," she muttered.

"Well, then, off you go, young Kes," One-Ear Tom said, sending her down the slope with a gentle push. She had not taken a dozen strides when he called out, "Remember who you are, and what you've done to get here, and you'll be fine." His worried expression did nothing to assure her, so she turned and made her way down the slope.

When she reached the ring of villagers, they parted, all looking at her as if she was already a hero. She did not understand their adoration any more than she understood why the suggestion kept coming up that she had done anything more than any other Potential.

Kestrel ducked her head and pushed through them, then passed the ring of Red Hands. She did not stop until she reached the calm center of the two rings formed by the villagers and the warriors.

All around her drums pounded in rough

harmony with the clacking of wooden weapons. The Red Hands circled and circled, their mock battles lively. No one seemed to be paying Kestrel any mind, but she sensed watchful eyes, sensed the silent question held within every head. *Who will she challenge?*

Like her, they all knew this was only meant to be a demonstration of a newly raised Red Hand's skills, but it was still great fun to watch.

I will give them a show they will never forget, she thought, and abruptly thrust one of her wooden knives skyward. "See me!"

At that signal, the drumming and the fighting ceased at once. Everyone locked their eyes on her. She gazed back, forcing herself to hold her head high and proud.

She gripped the leather-wrapped hilts of her wooden knives tightly. When she breathed in, it seemed as though she was drawing strength from her people. Excitement overflowed her veins and spilled into the rest of her body, making her tremble like the leaves of an aspen tree. Before the trembling could become visible shaking, she snapped her heels together and crossed her practice weapons before her face in salute.

Who will she challenge? Hundreds of eager eyes asked, but the time had not yet come to reveal her choice.

Kestrel leaped forward, once and again, gaining

speed with each bound, until she was flying around the clearing, her blades spinning around her head in a whirring, intermingled pattern, feeling alive with joy and purpose.

Her third time around the ring, her leaping strides suddenly transformed into a series of high, spinning kicks, each punctuated by a shout of, "*Ha!*" Each time her feet lit upon the ground, she slashed and stabbed at an enemy none of the observers could see—the Stone Dogs on the mountain. Lost as she was in this dance of blades, she could see them as clearly as she had on that stormy night after her Kill.

In her mind, they came at her in ones and twos, ugly beasts of men, their hair and beards teased into ratty, sodden ropes, their spears stabbing but unable to touch her, as she blocked and spun away, and then spun back again to strike them down. She could actually feel the cold rain pounding against her skin; hear the howling voice of the storm mingling with the screams of her enemies. Eight had chased after her, but she found only seven to cut down. *Where is the other?*

Kestrel faltered imperceptibly at the thought, threw herself forward into a diving somersault, and came up again, her wooden blades hissing as they cut the air ... only the air.

The magic of the moment began to fade, and she finished her exhibition with a few more high kicks, followed by an equal number of sweeping kicks that would have knocked any enemy off their feet.

Breathing deeply, she stood straight, and once more snapped her heels together and crossed her blades before her face.

"Hear me!" she called this time.

Expectant faces peered at her. *Who will she challenge?*

Kestrel swallowed. She could still challenge One-Ear Tom, her father, or someone else, but there was only one. He had dogged her as long as she could remember, embarrassed and belittled her at every turn, and tonight, in some small way, no matter the cost, she meant to return some of that hurt and misery to him.

She stabbed one blade skyward, then let it fall slowly, until aimed at the target she had chosen. "I challenge Aiden, my brother, and the Warchief of my chosen band!"

Normally after the challenge was made, cheers erupted from the villagers and the Red Hands. Kestrel heard only the whispering of the breeze, the rustling of the grass underfoot, the faint rattle of bones hanging from the Bone Tree, and the distant *cree-cree* of crickets.

Hundreds of faces stared back, many with mouths hanging open. A few of the villagers looked to one another and shook their heads in bewilderment. *Has she lost her wits?* their expressions said. Before anyone could voice aloud that opinion, One-Ear Tom stepped forward.

"Will the challenged accept?" he called, his deep voice revealing not a hint of the doubt Kestrel saw from the villagers.

Wearing a broad, mocking grin, Aiden moved out of the ring of Red Hands. "I will, and gladly!"

Silence held a moment longer, then the drums began pounding again, the Red Hands sat themselves on the ground and crossed their legs. Though hesitant at first, the villagers offered up a thunderous cheer.

Kestrel stood firm as Aiden drew close, but the hilts of her weapons had become greasy with sweat, and she had to concentrate to keep a firm hold on them. *This is what you wanted,* she reminded herself. *Be strong, and honor yourself and your family.*

"I hope you don't expect me to be gentle?" Aiden asked out of the corner of his mouth, as he offered a nod and a wave to the spectators.

"You never have been before."

"For good reason," Aiden said quietly, his gray eyes meeting hers. "I told you before that your shortcomings would become obvious to everyone, but I didn't know you wanted to hurry things along."

He's toying with you, she thought, fury exploding within her chest. The time had come to make him choke on all the bitter, hateful things he had said and done to her.

"I wonder, will my brother fight?" she cried in a taunting voice. "Or will he talk us all to tears?"

When the villagers and the Red Hands gave a stirring roar of approval, an ugly light entered Aiden's stare.

One-Ear Tom lifted a hand for quiet. He flashed a smile, but Kestrel saw a ghost of worry hovering under it. "I don't know about the rest of you, but the night is growing late, and I'm getting hungry." He waited until the cheers died down, and added, "Let us begin!"

After he had stepped out of the ring, Kestrel and Aiden faced each other, set their feet, and held their weapons at the ready. The thought crossed Kestrel's mind to adjust her stance, and then Aiden attacked.

CHAPTER EIGHTEEN

Aiden was on her in two quick strides, his wooden blades twirling. Before she could so much as blink, one had thumped against the bandage on her shoulder, and the other cracked sharply against her wounded hip. The spectators' cheering became gasps. This part of the ceremony was supposed to display Kestrel's prowess, not make her look like a fool.

Kestrel stumbled back, teeth clenched against a pained groan. The dull, throbbing agony the seeker's tea had stolen from her wounds thundered back to life, for a moment making it impossible to think straight.

Aiden struck her twice again, once a hammering blow to her ribs, and another to one wrist. Her numbed fingers sprang open, and the wooden knife fell away. Before it hit the ground, his blades were falling again.

Move!

She obeyed the silent command just in time.

As Kestrel threw herself backward, one of

Aiden's blades ripped through the space where her head had been a split-second before, the blunted tip slicing the air in front her nose—had she not dodged clear, she would be sprawled on the ground with a cracked skull.

Does he mean to kill me? she thought, soaring out of reach. Before she hit the ground, Kestrel folded her arms across her chest and tucked her legs. After she hit, she let her momentum roll her over to her feet. She came up in a crouch, hoping the quick escape had put Aiden off his stride.

He was already closing, teeth bared, blades swinging.

Kestrel threw herself into another backward roll, but when she came up this time, she feinted one way, then ducked low in the opposite direction. As Aiden lunged past, her sidearm swing cracked loudly against his lower back, pulling a startled grunt from his throat.

Most of the villagers had lost their shock at seeing an actual fight break out between the siblings, and now they howled encouragement over the crazed pounding of drums. "Aiden!" many called out; considerably less shouted, "Kestrel!"

Not waiting for Aiden to gain the advantage, Kestrel surged across the clearing, caught up her fallen knife, and spun to face her brother.

He was already so close that she had to drop to her belly to avoid catching a wooden blade with her teeth. It whooshed overhead, skimming her flying braid. Aiden's momentum carried him along, and his boots tromped across her shoulders and down her spine.

Kestrel rolled to her back in time to avoid Aiden's next strike, which hammered a deep groove in the grass. She scissored her legs around and swept him off his feet. When he slammed down into the grass inches from her, she tried to drive her blade into his face. He caught the weapon with his own, and shoved it aside.

Scrambling and grunting, they both came up together. They circled each other warily, each panting like overheated dogs. The trickle of blood running from her brother's nose proclaimed that her last strike had landed, after all. The bellowing villagers bounced on their toes and waved their hands overhead, calling for more.

"Are you done playing, little sister?" Aiden growled, spinning his wooden knives in a showy flourish.

Kestrel dug a toe deep into the grass. "I am a Red Hand. I do not play."

"You are no Red—"

He cut off with a yell when Kestrel kicked a tuft of grass and dirt into his face. Clawing at his eyes, he spun away.

She followed, hammering one blade against his shoulder, the other against his ribs. Shaking his head and snarling, Aiden fell to one knee. Kestrel reared back, lifting her weapons high, meaning to crack his head.

Aiden had been waiting for the irresistible attack. As soon as she stretched up, exposing her middle, he lashed out. His fists, wrapped tight about the hilts of his knives, crashed against her belly, one after the other, driving the breath from her body and knocking her backward. Kestrel's arms pinwheeled, her feet tangled, and she went down in a twisted heap. Instinct alone made her get up, her head swinging wildly in search of her brother.

He was not where she expected. He had darted a quarter of the distance around the clearing, and was flashing near on her weak side, one blade held out before him, the other cocked behind his head.

She blocked the outthrust blade before he could stab it into her neck, and his second weapon instantly slashed down, glancing off the side of her head and cracking against her injured shoulder. As he flew by her, his foot collided with her chest, knocking her to her back.

Kestrel rolled woozily to her side, head lolling. Aiden, wooden knives held over his head in triumph, swaggered around the ring. The villagers bellowed their approval. Kestrel found her mother and father standing beside One-Ear Tom. Their expressions ranged from fear to disappointment to pity.

Fury caught fire within Kestrel, gave her the strength to get to her feet again. As Aiden continued to play the strutting rooster, she stood swaying, wooden knives held limply in her hands. Her ribs felt cracked. Blood swamped her mouth, a trickle dribbling from her lips. More ran from the bandages at her hip and neck. In that moment, she saw her mistakes. By falling prey to her desire for revenge against her brother, she had shamed the only person that mattered. *Herself.* Everyone would remember how she had failed this night, but what she would remember was how she had proven Aiden right about not being fit to be a Red Hand.

No, she thought. Then, with more force, *NO!*

Play the rabbit, One-Ear Tom and Tessa said as one within her mind.

To defeat the wolf, she had no choice.

When Aiden returned his attention to her, he flashed a merciless grin and stalked close, gaining speed with every step. His blades whirled.

Come to me, wolf.

At the last instant, Kestrel threw her arms high, as if stricken with terror and meaning to surrender. Scalding tears threatened to overspill her eyes, and she let them fall.

Aiden's pace increased.

Kestrel abruptly lowered her blades. Seeing her ploy, Aiden tried to turn aside, but he was too close, coming too fast, and he rammed against their wooden tips. He grunted sharply when they dug into his belly. Kestrel locked one arm and folded the other, spinning Aiden off balance. She shoved hard, and sent him sprawling facedown.

Before he could leap up, Kestrel brought both blades down on the back of his head, splitting his scalp in two places and slamming his face against the ground.

Stunned silence fell for the second time that night.

Before victory could escape, Kestrel leaped on Aiden's back, slid the edge of one wooden knife under his throat, and caught the tip with her other hand. Aiden convulsed, trying to buck her off, but Kestrel pulled hard, grinding the blade against his neck. She had only to pull a little harder to crush his windpipe. He went still, his rapid breaths gurgling and strained.

"Do you surrender, brother?" she hissed.

Instead of answering directly, Aiden twisted his head. Blood was pouring from his nose and split lips, and there were bits of grass stuck to his face. He surprised her by rasping, loud enough for all to hear, "I'm beaten. Please, little sister, have mercy!"

As the villagers erupted, Kestrel felt Aiden shuddering, and eased the blade from his neck. She looked again at his bloody face, and was shocked to find that he was laughing.

Before she could even begin to wonder what he

thought was so funny, the villagers lifted her above their heads and carried her on a surging wave back up the knoll to the Bone Tree.

CHAPTER NINETEEN

Kestrel felt dazed and distant from all that had happened. The seeker's tea, gaining the mark of a Red Hand, displaying her fighting skills alone and against Aiden, and finally the crazed, bouncing journey back up the knoll in the hands of her exuberant people, all seemed like parts of a peculiar dream that fit poorly together.

And now, once more, she found herself standing beneath the Bone Tree. Only one thing remained before the tribe recognized her as a Red Hand, but she had a hard time focusing on it.

Sweat, dirt, and blood covered her head to toe, and tufts of dead grass hung from her hair. She hurt all over, and each heartbeat thumped in her ears, taking the place of the drums that had fallen as silent as the watching villagers. The taste of blood on her tongue made her queasy, and she worried, here at the last, that she would finally vomit in front of everyone.

Somehow, she swallowed the rising bile; somehow, she lifted her head and looked straight ahead.

An engraved box made of aged pine sat on the black and white stone bench between her and the Elders, who were braced on either side by the Warchiefs. Her father gave her a reserved grin and shook his head, as if to say, *My daughter, whatever will I do with you?*

With some effort, she shrugged meekly, and thought, *Let me sleep, I hope.*

Aiden stood among the Warchiefs and the Elders, looking as battered as she did. She did not for a minute believe skill had let her win the contest between them, but luck only. Had they really been fighting, Aiden's initial attack would have crippled or killed her immediately. When the day came when she fought a true battle, she would remember what had happened tonight, and be better prepared.

At her back, her mother was hidden amongst the rest of the Red Hands and the villagers, who had all pressed in close, but remained silent, listening intently to catch every detail of the ceremony's conclusion.

Kestrel began to think if things did not hurry up, she was going to have to sit down. If that shamed her in some way, so be it.

It was then that One-Ear Tom came forward with her father at his side. Where Matthias put on a solemn expression, Kestrel's mentor favored her with a pleased smile. Her father spoke first.

"On this night, the Ancestors have blessed all of us with another worthy protector. That Kestrel is my daughter, and my second child to prove she has the ability and fortitude to serve us as a Red Hand, only blesses me that much more."

The villagers matched the Elder's gravity with a low rumble of approval that made Kestrel feel loved and grateful. From this night forward, her sole purpose would be to defend these people at all costs, a task she had wanted all her life. Tears of gladness welled in her eyes.

"Now," her father went on, as One-Ear Tom opened the lid of the box and reached inside, "let these bones we hang upon the tree of our Ancestors, and those we hang around her neck, prove to one and all that my daughter, Kestrel Stoneheart, has fulfilled all the demands required of her to join those who defend our lives against our enemies."

The murmurs of approval were louder this time, sprinkled with clapping from the women, and chest pounding from the men.

For Kestrel, what her father was saying, and the response from the villagers, had grown distant. Her eyes had locked on the necklace One-Ear Tom took out of the box. There was something wrong with it. The lion's teeth were clear enough—four of them, long and sharp, strung on a stout leather cord. But there were other teeth on the cord, as well. Human teeth.

As One-Ear Tom stepped around the bench and came closer to her, holding the necklace out before him, Matthias reached inside the box. Instead of pulling out one skull, two came out. In his right hand, he held the lion's skull. It had been stripped of all flesh and hide, and gleamed a creamy yellow in the torchlight. In his left hand, he held a human skull, which also shone with a buttery hue. The top of each had been fitted with a short length of wire and a brass clip. As he raised them up for all to see, an awed murmur went through the crowd.

Kestrel stared at the human skull, a low buzzing sound filling her head. *What is this?* Before she could work up enough spit to loosen her tongue, her father spoke again.

"When my son, Aiden, became the youngest Red Hand by taking a Black Ear as his Kill, I never expected to see his achievement bested. Apparently, my daughter saw fit to follow his example. Not content with slaying a fierce lion, she also pursued and killed one of our vilest foes." He hefted the skull. "Thankfully, this particular Stone Dog will never join another raiding party against us."

The cheer that erupted from the villagers was deafening, and despite the formality of the ceremony, dozens of people surged forward, all reaching out to touch Kestrel, as though she were a living talisman that could change the fortune of their lives. At that moment she understood her mother's strange edginess earlier, and also her father's look of pride.

If One-Ear Tom had not arrived at that moment and placed the necklace around her neck, Kestrel would have fallen over. As he backed away, an idea struck her that made more sense than anything else did. *I am dreaming. I'm lying somewhere up on the mountain, feverish and dying from flesh-rot.*

Her father raised his hands, quieting the villagers. "To all those Potentials who seek to become Red Hands in the future, I give this warning. Do not think you must prove yourself better than my children." Unable to hide his proud look, he added sternly, "Once you become a Red Hand in the *usual* way, there will be plenty of opportunity to face our enemies. Doing so before you are ready, even if you *think* you are ready, or worse yet, because you *think* you should, will only result in far fewer Potentials returning home with their Kill. Is that understood?"

The villagers accepted his words of caution by laughing loudly, and slapping the backs of the few young, blushing Potentials.

Kestrel peered about. None of this felt like a dream, yet she knew she had not killed any of the Stone Dogs who had chased her....

Her silent denial drifted way like so much thistledown, along with the rowdy villagers. And

135

then she was on the mountain again, only a few steps ahead of rough men howling for her blood, sprinting through darkness slashed with pulses of lightning, the trees around her whipped by wind and rain.

She saw the hazy outline of a man rise up before her, saw herself lifting her knife and locking her elbow, turning her arm into a spear. A second later, she collided with him and bounced away. When she got to her feet, the knife was gone from her hand, and her enemy was making *breathless* gagging noises. She might have knocked the wind from him, or....

Or did I bury my blade in his chest?

It seemed possible, even likely.

The memory danced away, and another took its place.

She was sitting on the soggy ground across the fire from Aiden, angry and hurt after listening to him tell her how honorless and weak she was, but she was also frustrated because he refused to believe the number of men she had seen—eight on the mountain, and another lying in wait at the edge of the forest....

Another shift, backward, to the moment Aiden attacked the Stone Dogs, his blades whistling through the rainy night air as easily as they cut through the men. They fell, one by one, and she counted them now, as she had then. The number remained the same. Seven dead. Seven Stone Dogs. Not eight or nine, but *seven*....

Another shift, forward to the moment before they set out for the river. *A true Red Hand, little sister, never loses their weapon,* Aiden had said, and then hurled a knife into the ground beside her hip. The knife her father had given her; the knife she had lost. There was only one possible way Aiden could have retrieved it.

While I was unconscious, he must've gone back up the mountain. Kestrel clearly imagined him ghosting through the sodden forest, a shadow among shadows, until he came to the fallen man— *The man I stabbed ... the man I* killed.

Kestrel blinked away the images in time to see her father and One-Ear Tom move under the Bone Tree. After nodding to each other, they each grasped a nearly invisible wire—which a Red Hand or two had strung through the branches, and who were even now hidden out of sight—and clipped the skulls to the looped ends. As the two old warriors stepped back, the hidden Red Hands slowly drew the two skulls aloft, stopping when they dangled twenty feet up.

Kestrel stared along with everyone else, but her mind had snagged on another detail: *How did I bring the skull of the Stone Dog home without knowing it?*

The answer came swiftly.

Aiden had found her knife, and when he did, he had also taken the Stone Dog's head, and then hid it within his knapsack. Later, somewhere outside the village, Aiden must have placed the Kill in her hands. The bundled, bloody hide had *seemed* heavier and larger, because it *had* been. With the same eerie clarity as before, she saw herself lolling about on a night-shadowed forest trail, caught in the throes of delirium, while Aiden stole a sly glance her way, then carefully wrapped the skulls of man and beast together in the lion's hide....

A final question bubbled to the surface, and it troubled her more than everything else. Why would Aiden make her a hero amongst her people?

Before she found a suitable answer, the stillness of those around her brought her back into the moment.

Matthias and One-Ear Tom stood looking at her, quizzical frowns wrinkling their brows. One-Ear Tom's lips moved, but the buzzing in Kestrel's head had returned, a sound like countless flies swarming within a tiny cave.

Others were looking her way now, some with patient smiles, some with concern, but most with guarded alarm, as if something about her expression worried them.

"What did you see, young Kes?" One-Ear Tom said, his voice pushing through the droning in her head.

I cannot tell you. Kestrel swallowed, ran her leather-dry tongue around her mouth, and raised a tentative finger to the teeth hung on her necklace. Lion teeth. Human teeth. All in a row, cool against her neck.

Her mentor tried again, leaning forward, peering intently at her. She saw herself reflected in his pupils, and behind her dozens of frozen faces. "What did the Ancestors show you?" His lips spread in a tentative smile. "Come girl, tell us, so that we can get on with feasting, and you can get some rest."

"The Ancestors?" Kestrel rasped, stupid with confusion. What did the Ancestors have to do with any of this? "I ... I don't understand."

One-Ear Tom glanced sharply at Matthias. "She came too soon to the ceremony. We should have waited. "

He spoke under his breath, but Kestrel heard him as plainly as if he had shouted. Her eyes rolled in her head until they landed on Aiden. He wore a self-satisfied expression that made no more sense than anything else.

"Ask her again," Matthias said.

One-Ear Tom nodded hesitantly. "When you drank the seeker's tea, Kestrel," he said, speaking every word precisely, "did the Ancestors show you anything that might help our people?"

Kestrel looked back to Aiden, but now he would not meet her gaze. *What have you done?*

"Kestrel Stoneheart! What did the Ancestors show you?"

Startled by her teacher's shout, Kestrel forced herself to concentrate. Had the Ancestors *shown* her anything? She thought there *was* one thing that had happened after she drank the seeker's tea that had not happened in real life. Could that be the message One-Ear Tom wanted to hear?

Say nothing about this, Aiden had warned in the old city, and in her mind tonight, when the seeker's tea had filled her with so many strange sensations.

You do not frighten me. I am a Red Hand, she had responded in the vision, the words bursting from her in the form of a shimmering blast that struck Aiden in the chest and exploded him into a cloud of dust.

Did the Ancestors want her to kill Aiden with something that looked like a blast from a firelance pistol? That made no sense!

Kestrel shook her head, trying to understand—

She could almost hear the click in her mind when everything fell into place.

The old city. The stock of firelance pistols Aiden intended to use against the Tall Ones. And the last thing, the power of her words rendering him harmless.... Was that a sign from the Ancestors telling her that they would protect her if she revealed the truth he wanted kept hidden?

140

It must be.

The thought was half hope, half certainty.

When I tell, everyone will object to Aiden's mad scheme.... Ancestors, protect me.

Kestrel looked directly at Aiden. "The will of the Ancestors is for me to join my brother in making war against the Tall Ones."

Shocked silence held for a moment, before a frenzied uproar swept through the villagers. And for the second time that night, her brother burst out laughing.

CHAPTER TWENTY

One-Ear Tom moved swiftly to haul Kestrel away from the villagers, and then placed her behind the black and white stone bench for good measure. Looking at the faces of her people, some livid, some shocked, she wondered if the Ancestors had played a cruel trick on her.

Some villagers had pushed forward, waving fists, demanding answers, but most had retreated, faces tight with fear at the idea of attacking the reclusive Tall Ones. Anytime something bad or unusual happened, the Tall Ones were blamed. If a child died in the womb, or someone vanished, or if a drought or flood destroyed the crops, or if the game herds were thinner one year, stories swept through the village, whisperings of just-glimpsed phantoms, or strange lights, or any number of odd occurrences. There were many reasons no one had ever made war against those people—or monsters, as most believed—but the most prominent reason, if never admitted aloud, was fear.

"Quiet!" her father called, glaring. "I assure

you, my daughter is mistaken. She has earned great honor among us with her deeds, but at great cost. She needs rest. After she has had time to heal, she can reveal the true will of the Ancestors."

That calmed people down, and many nodded eagerly, but then Aiden broke away from his band, his smile and laughter gone, replaced by a look of grave certainty.

"She is not wrong," he said, leaping up onto the bench, and then hauled Kestrel up to stand at his side.

"I will hear no more of this nonsense!" Matthias bellowed. "Both of you, get down from there!"

Kestrel moved to obey, but Aiden held her in place. "What do you fear, father? What do any of you fear?" he asked, sweeping his gaze over the villagers.

"The living cannot fight evil spirits! It is madness!" One-Ear Tom declared, earning a few calls of agreement.

Aiden spoke up. "Who are any of us to refute the will of the Ancestors?"

"We are not *refuting* the Ancestors," Matthias said, "only the words of a girl who barely made it back to the village alive, and who is obviously still suffering from her trials."

"This *suffering girl* beat me in a fair contest," Aiden retorted, lifting his chin to show the red mark on his neck, then turning to display the blood beginning to dry on the back of his shaved scalp. He did not need to add that beating him was no small feat. Everyone knew it, and Kestrel could see the renewed flashes of wonder in their eyes when they glanced her way.

Despite a surge of pride at what she had done, she knew her brother had planned everything that had happened tonight, even if she could not guess why. Aiden went on.

"What Kes *saw* is exactly what the Ancestors *showed* her, and only fools and cowards would dare balk at the will of those who watch over and guide us. I am neither a fool nor a coward. Nor is my sister. My hope," he finished, his gray eyes touching each face, "is that none of you are, either."

A chorus of affirming yells went up, but halfhearted at best. No one wanted to be counted a fool or a coward, but it was also apparent that none of them could understand why the Ancestors would have them make war against the Tall Ones, a terrible enemy that even the crazed Black Ears avoided.

"Even if this is the will of the Ancestors," Matthias said slowly, "the Elders and the Warchiefs must discuss this matter further, unless—" his eyes shifted to Kestrel "—the Ancestors gave you a strategy?"

Kestrel looked upon her father and her brother,

the other Elders and Warchiefs, then the expectant faces of her people. She felt caught in a rushing stream, tumbled and turned, her mouth and throat filling with thick, muddy water. She wished she could begin the day over—truth told, she wished she could turn back time to the moment she had first stepped out of the village to begin her hunt for the Kill. But such ability was beyond her, so all she could do was shake her head.

"Very well," Matthias continued. "For now, we will feast in honor of our newest Red Hand, Kestrel, my daughter."

The villagers leaped at this opportunity, as if they had been waiting for a way to escape the discussion. Kestrel watched them break quickly into chattering groups. Just short of running, they dispersed across the knoll, torches bouncing in their hands, the children darting and laughing, unaware of what all the fuss was about, all heading to the edge of the clearing where food and firewood had been stored earlier in preparation for the feast. Even the Warchiefs fled, leaving only the Elders, Kestrel, and her brother.

"Father," Aiden called. "If we deny the will of the Ancestors, no matter what our hearts tell us is the right thing to do, it will, in time, ruin the faith of our people."

Matthias studied his son for a long time before speaking. "The moment you became a Warchief, you have wanted to attack the Tall Ones." Learning that the Elders had known all along of Aiden's plan made Kestrel feel as if someone had clubbed her, but Matthias was not finished. "I find it troubling that now your sister claims the same."

"It is not her *claim*," Aiden corrected. He glanced her way, his expression unreadable. "Or am I wrong?"

Kestrel hesitated. Earlier she had believed the Ancestors had shown her a vision about how to overcome her brother ... but what if they really wanted her to join Aiden? Before she could make sense of all that had happened, let alone find a way to say it, her father spoke again.

"We will discuss this later," Matthias said.

"We can discuss it all we want," Aiden countered, "but we cannot deceive ourselves. Our future is war, as decreed by the Ancestors."

"No one is deceiving themselves," Matthias said, sounding doubtful. "Now, go join the feast."

If there was any doubt that he was finished discussing the issue, he abruptly joined his peers and together they moved away with their heads bent together. One-Ear Tom glanced at Kestrel once, his features unreadable. Kestrel knew the Elders would gather after the feast and argue long into the night.

She scowled at her brother. "What are you playing at?"

He favored her with his usual sneer. "I have no

idea what you mean."

"Why did you really help me against the Stone Dogs?"

"Can't a brother aid his sister?"

"You never have before! Besides that, you were not supposed to help me. It is forbidden. You were supposed to observe, nothing more."

He shrugged. "I've known for some time that I needed someone else to help me convince the Elders, as well as our people, about what they must do. Then I looked at the least likely person … *you*."

Kestrel's frustration mounted to the point that her head felt ready to burst. "What does that mean?"

"You heard father. I've been trying to convince the Elders how dangerous the Tall Ones are since I became a Warchief. They listened to my warnings, then they made excuses, sounding wise and reasoned. But I know the real reason they hesitate—they are cowards. I had no choice but to use *you* to help me bring them around, and the Bone Tree ceremony was the best time to do that."

Kestrel narrowed her eyes. "The only way I could help is if you knew what the Ancestors would show me." She hesitated. "*Did* you know?"

Aiden laughed. "You really believe I'm so favored?" His smug expression suggested that he believed he should be. "No, Kes, I didn't know what they would reveal, any more than you could have known. My plans had nothing to do with the

Ancestors. I only intended to make you into a champion, someone who could rival even me, and then convince you to help me stir everyone else to action."

"I would never have agreed to help you do that!"

"Of course you wouldn't have—not my precious little sister! But when you grew feverish, I saw an opportunity to turn you into my champion by going back and retrieving the Stone Dog's head. It was a gamble, I admit, and there at the end when Father brought both skulls out of the box, I thought sure my gamble had failed. I was certain you would tell everyone that this entire ceremony had been a farce. But you kept quiet."

The shame burning in her cheeks spoke louder than any words she might have said, or any excuse she might have made. She had believed the Ancestors were showing her a way to turn everyone against him and his ridiculous plan.

Her brother added, "When you told of what the Ancestors showed you, I was as surprised as everyone else." A strange, feverish light came into his gray eyes. "But at the same time, Kes, I knew at that moment that I had been right all along: the Ancestors *want* us to go to war against the Tall Ones."

Kestrel felt as if the world were spinning around her. Could it be true? Did the Ancestors, who she felt sure had accepted the blood she offered in exchange for aid during the rite of the Kill, actually want her people to make war against the Tall Ones?

She did not want to believe it, but denying the apparent truth was impossible. The Ancestors had spoken through her, and their will must be done, even if she could not understand it.

All of it came down to a single, undeniable certainty. Sometime soon, in order to obey and keep the favor of the Ancestors, her people would make war on the Tall Ones.

So ends
Tribe - Part One: The Red Hand

If you enjoyed this book, please consider posting a helpful online review at Amazon. I would greatly appreciate it, as would future fans!

For all my current fans, thank you so much for reading, and I can't wait to continue the adventure with you!
~Kaelyn

Can't Wait For The Next Book?!

Tribe: Part Two: The Ghosts of Yesterday

Coming mid-January 2015!

Be sure to check for updates about the release date on my blog and Facebook page:

http://kaelynrossbooks.blogspot.com/

http://www.facebook.com/pages/Kaelyn-Ross/1570875296481518?ref=hl

About the Author

Kaelyn is a full-time young adult author who loves just about everything! Some of her favorites, though, are playing with her Mini-Schnauzer Max, riding her horse Annie, and cuddling with her husband (who is quite forgiving of all the horse hair when they cuddle!). She loves to travel and meet new people, and to hike the mountains near her home in beautiful Montana.